W9-BNP-462

BUZZ AROUND THE TRACK
They Said It

"I've been through bad, rotten and downright intolerable, but to get the job of my dreams I'll have to survive the interview of my worst nightmares…and a boss who is totally, absolutely and undeniably my type."
—Stacy Evans

"Stacy has curiosity. She has drive. And she blushes easily. But is she qualified to train our team?"
—Nathan Cargill

"Nathan Cargill is filling the shoes his father left behind. Our team needs his expertise…and his full attention."
—Dean Grosso

"Stacy's got some newfangled ideas about the training of our pit crew. If I have anything to say about it, she won't be here next month."
—Harley Mickowski

DORIEN KELLY

is a former attorney who is much happier as an author. In addition to her years practicing business law, at one point or another she has also been a waitress, a bank teller and a professional chauffeur to her three children. Her current (and very romantic) day job is executive director of a lighthouse keepers association.

When Dorien isn't writing or keeping lighthouses lit, she loves to garden, travel and be with her friends and family. A RITA® Award nominee, she is also the winner of a Romance Writers of America's Golden Heart Award, a Booksellers' Best Award, a Maggie Award and a Gayle Wilson Award of Excellence. She lives in a small village in Michigan with one or more of her children, the love of her life (when he can be home) and three crazed dogs.

NASCAR

OVER THE WALL

Dorien Kelly

HARLEQUIN®

TORONTO • NEW YORK • LONDON
AMSTERDAM • PARIS • SYDNEY • HAMBURG
STOCKHOLM • ATHENS • TOKYO • MILAN • MADRID
PRAGUE • WARSAW • BUDAPEST • AUCKLAND

If you purchased this book without a cover you should be aware
that this book is stolen property. It was reported as "unsold and
destroyed" to the publisher, and neither the author nor the
publisher has received any payment for this "stripped book."

Recycling programs
for this product may
not exist in your area.

ISBN-13: 978-0-373-18523-8

OVER THE WALL

Copyright © 2009 by Harlequin Books S.A.

Dorien Kelly is acknowledged as the author of this work.

NASCAR® and the NASCAR Library Collection® are registered
trademarks of the National Association for Stock Car Auto Racing, Inc.

All rights reserved. Except for use in any review, the reproduction or
utilization of this work in whole or in part in any form by any electronic,
mechanical or other means, now known or hereafter invented, including
xerography, photocopying and recording, or in any information storage
or retrieval system, is forbidden without the written permission of the
publisher, Harlequin Enterprises Limited, 225 Duncan Mill Road,
Don Mills, Ontario, Canada M3B 3K9.

This is a work of fiction. Names, characters, places and incidents are
either the product of the author's imagination or are used fictitiously,
and any resemblance to actual persons, living or dead, business
establishments, events or locales is entirely coincidental.

This edition published by arrangement with Harlequin Books S.A.

® and TM are trademarks of the publisher. Trademarks indicated with
® are registered in the United States Patent and Trademark Office, the
Canadian Trade Marks Office and in other countries.

www.eHarlequin.com

Printed in U.S.A.

For Marsha Zinberg.
Thanks once again for giving me the opportunity to learn!

NASCAR HIDDEN LEGACIES

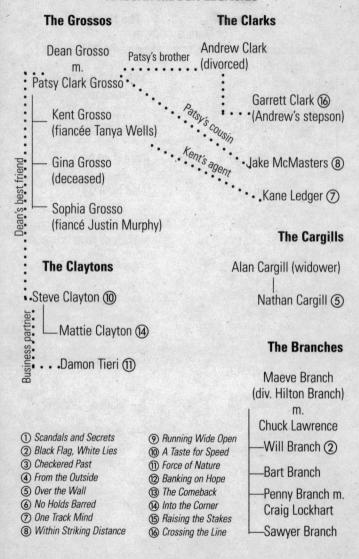

The Grossos

Dean Grosso
m.
Patsy Clark Grosso

— Kent Grosso
(fiancée Tanya Wells)

— Gina Grosso
(deceased)

— Sophia Grosso
(fiancé Justin Murphy)

The Claytons

— Steve Clayton ⑩

    └ Mattie Clayton ⑭

— Damon Tieri ⑪

Patsy's brother

Patsy's cousin

Kent's agent

Dean's best friend

Business partner

The Clarks

Andrew Clark
(divorced)

Garrett Clark ⑯
(Andrew's stepson)

Jake McMasters ⑧

Kane Ledger ⑦

The Cargills

Alan Cargill (widower)
|
Nathan Cargill ⑤

The Branches

Maeve Branch
(div. Hilton Branch)
m.
Chuck Lawrence

— Will Branch ②

— Bart Branch

— Penny Branch m.
Craig Lockhart

— Sawyer Branch

THE FAMILIES AND THE CONNECTIONS

The Sanfords

Bobby Sanford · · · · · · · · · · · · Dan Hunt
(deceased)
m.
Kath Sanford

— Adam Sanford ①

— Brent Sanford ⑫

— Trey Sanford ⑨

The Hunts

m.
Linda (Willard) Hunt
(deceased)

— Ethan Hunt ⑥

— Jared Hunt ⑮

— Hope Hunt ⑫

— Grace Hunt Winters ⑯
(widow of Todd Winters)

The Mathesons

Brady Matheson
(widower)
(fiancée Julie-Anne Blake)

— Chad Matheson ③

— Zack Matheson ⑬

— Trent Matheson
(fiancée Kelly Greenwood)

The Daltons

Buddy Dalton
m.
Shirley Dalton

— Mallory Dalton ④

— Tara Dalton ①

— Emma-Lee Dalton

CHAPTER ONE

STACY EVANS CHECKED her makeup for the third time since pulling into the parking lot at Cargill-Grosso Racing. Cosmetics were low on her list of worries, but at least they were something she could control. The butterflies on caffeine flitting around in her stomach clearly had minds of their own. There would be no taming them until she exited this job interview.

Stacy wanted the team's newly posted position as Kent Grosso's pit crew strength and conditioning coach so very much. Too much, really. While she loved NASCAR and the excitement that swirled around it, that wasn't the big reason she was here. The personal stuff, though, she had to push aside if she had any hope at all of remaining collected through her talk with team manager Nathan Cargill. With her lack of an exercise physiology degree—heck, any kind of a college degree, for that matter—she was lucky to have been asked to interview.

Sure that her mascara hadn't produced a single stray fleck, that her lip gloss was perfectly applied, and that she wasn't about to commit one of those interview atrocities of giving a direct and sincere speech about her qualifications with a bit of her morning granola stuck between her teeth, she turned her rearview mirror back into position. Before exiting the car, Stacy spoke her employment mantra.

"Overdeliver," she said in a firm voice.

So far, that mantra had given her the confidence and drive to escape the dark chaos that had been life growing up with Brenda, her mother, and to move up from being an assistant at a crowded Charlotte gym to having her own packed list of wealthy, private clients who swore that Stacy was a miracle-working fitness trainer.

Overdeliver. What else could a girl do? Except maybe fail, and no way on earth would she do that. She'd watched her mother fail, and it had been an ugly lesson that she had no intention of repeating.

Stacy exited Maude, her beloved rust bucket of a vehicle, then opened the sedan's back door to extract the slim leather portfolio that contained additional copies of her résumé and letters of reference, plus a little something that she hoped would clinch the job for her. She had prepared days for this interview, scouring the Internet for all the information she could obtain on other racing teams' strength and conditioning coaches, and their failures and successes, not to mention all the info she could dig up on Kent Grosso's pit crew. She had come up with what she believed were the optimal set of exercises to focus on each crew member's core strength. And to bolster her confidence, she had splurged on a new, trim navy-blue suit, one that accented her athletic shape without flaunting her other attributes, which were often too apparent for her own comfort.

Although it was still early—just before nine on a

sunny North Carolina springtime day—the Cargill-Grosso lot held its share of tourists anxious to look into No. 414's shop, and maybe even get a glimpse of driver Kent Grosso, or his dad, NASCAR legend and new team owner, Dean. Plenty of fans milled in front of No. 507's shop, too. Driver Roberto Castillo might be new to NASCAR, but his prior open-wheel racing wins had given him immediate notice.

To the left of the garages sat the small museum and gift shop. She'd been there as a fan, but would be skipping them today. Instead, she walked to another long and low-slung building that she knew held most of the administrative offices. Before stepping under the shady portico, Stacy paused for three deep, cleansing breaths. Maybe it was a little odd that a high-energy girl thrived on yoga, but she figured there were worse personality quirks out there.

The building's reception area was empty, except for a receptionist. She smiled up at Stacy from her seat behind a mahogany reception desk.

"Good morning," she said.

Stacy was afraid that her answering smile was a little nervous around the edges. "Hi, I'm Stacy Evans. I have a nine-o'clock appointment with Nathan Cargill."

The receptionist checked the computer monitor in front of her, then said, "Welcome, Ms. Evans. If you'd please sign in, I'll let Mr. Cargill know you're here."

While the receptionist phoned Nathan Cargill's office, Stacy took in some details. Shiny brass letters on the wall behind the reception desk proclaimed Cargill-Grosso Racing. If she'd had a second longer to snoop, she would have checked out the framed photographs over by the shiny—and quite filled—trophy cabinet to see if Nathan Cargill was in any of them. The few photos she'd seen of him on the Internet were of the business variety, as though he'd switched off his soul just before the camera's shutter had clicked. Based on those pictures, were she to pin one word on the man, it would be *unapproachable*.

"Ms. Evans," the receptionist said. "You'll find Mr. Cargill and Mr. Noble down that hallway, in the first conference room on your left."

Mr. Noble?

Stacy felt her butterflies kick into high gear. While it made good sense that Kent Grosso's crew chief, Perry Noble, would be involved in the decision, no one had mentioned that he'd be in the interview. Much like Nathan Cargill, Perry Noble had a reputation as an exacting man. Both Cargill and Noble in the same room smacked of a "bad cop/worse cop" kind of interview.

"Thank you," Stacy said to the receptionist.

As she followed the other woman's directions, Stacy pulled back her shoulders, pinned on a smile and prepared to do battle. Heaven knows she'd survived worse.

The door to the conference room was slightly ajar… just enough that she could see Nathan Cargill seated at the far end of the long conference table, with Perry Noble to his left. As she took in Nathan Cargill's features, her butterflies suddenly lurched to a halt and then began a new dance. This one shimmied with the rhythm of attraction. Stupid butterflies.

Stacy had never thought about whether she had a "type" of man that attracted her. Now, with no thought at all, she knew. Nathan Cargill was totally, absolutely and undeniably her type. His dark hair was perfectly cut, and his gray eyes danced with amusement at something Perry Noble had just said. But his smile remained reserved, as though it was something he didn't bring out too often. Down to the knot in what she imagined had to be a very expensive silk tie, he was elegant…and hot. Definitely hot. He bore the stamp of one of those incredibly rich power brokers who could change the course of countless lives with one swipe of his pen.

She clutched her portfolio a little tighter in her left hand and prepared to knock…once she stopped shaking.

"You may come in, Ms. Evans," he said in a deep voice before she'd had the opportunity to quell even one of those butterflies.

Oh crap! Had he been watching her gawk at him all this time?

As STACY EVANS ENTERED the room, Nathan assessed what he knew about her thus far…the important things. Things that a résumé could never divulge, but observation could. She had curiosity, which he considered a good thing in an employee. Except when that employee was spying on him, as Ms. Evans just had.

She clearly had drive. Her stride as she came to the far end of the room was longer than one would expect of someone her height. Take away the stilettos she was wearing, and he'd put her at five foot four, at best. Still, she carried herself as though she'd topped out at six feet.

Finally, she blushed easily, which meant she cared what others thought of her. She would have a tough time conning him, too, with the way her every thought shone through her blue eyes. Since he was all about team and team play, he'd put both of those attributes on the good side of her ledger. On the whole, none of that fully balanced against the fact that without a college degree, she was grossly underqualified in an academic sense. Still, after checking her references, he'd been curious enough about her to invite her to interview.

Nathan rose as she neared. He noted that Perry hadn't bothered to do the same. It was a small thing, but it annoyed Nathan. Whatever conflicts the team might have should stay within the team and never be seen by the outside world. Perry had already made it abundantly clear that he thought Harley Mickowski, the pit crew coach and one of the team's top mechanics, too, was doing an acceptable job in making sure the crew was fit. The numbers showed that Perry was wrong. Common sense said that if the over-the-wall pit crew followed Harley's exercise regime, they were going to be in a world of hurt. While as sharp as they came when dealing with the physical mechanics of a pit stop, Harley had made friends with a few too many cheeseburgers.

Ms. Evans, on the other hand, was fit. Very fit.

She held her hand out to him. "I'm Stacy Evans, which you already know. Just as I know you're Nathan Cargill," she added with a smile.

If she'd been rattled coming in the door, she had done a great job of recovering.

"Hello, Ms. Evans," he said, shaking her hand. He'd been right about her height. If she were barefoot, he'd wager that she was almost a foot shorter than he. She was a knockout, though. Not his type—he preferred

Harvard MBAs with their glossy exteriors and sharp wits—but a knockout nonetheless.

"Ms. Evans, this is Kent's crew chief, Perry Noble," Nathan said. "He'll be sitting in on the interview." That was intended as a nudge at Perry, to remind him that he'd lost all decision-making power on this issue when he'd decided to do an end run to Dean and Patsy Grosso. Big mistake, since Dean and his wife and business partner, Patsy, had seen the need for improved physical training on the No. 414 over-the-wall pit crew as clearly as Nathan had.

Stacy went around the table and held out her hand to the crew chief. "It's a pleasure to meet you, Mr. Noble. I don't often get to meet a NASCAR legend."

Nathan bit back a smile as Perry stood and shook their latest interviewee's hand while giving a gruff hello. Even Perry had to cave a little under the woman's sincerity.

"Why don't you have a seat opposite Mr. Noble?" Nathan suggested as he sat.

When she'd had a chance to settle in, he pulled his copy of her résumé from his folder and watched as she provided Perry with an extra copy. Add *prepared* to her list of attributes. He'd been surprised by the number of interviewees they'd seen who'd apparently decided to try to wing it.

"I don't know if you're much of a NASCAR follower, Ms. Evans," Nathan began to say.

"Oh, I am. I've been following it for years!"

He gave her a few extra points for enthusiasm. His father's entire existence had centered around his team and NASCAR. Nathan's, far less so. Since his father's murder six months ago, Nathan had been acting as team manager for the Grossos until Dean and Patsy could find someone to fill the position. Although he'd grown to love NASCAR more and more, daily, Nathan grew more impatient to get back to his consultancy business in Boston. But this was his job for now, and he would give it his full attention.

"Then you have probably read the articles about Kent's less than stellar performance this season," he said to Ms. Evans. "Some of that is going to come with the fact that, except for Perry, most everyone is new this season. The pit crew lacks cohesiveness. The pit stop time has been creeping steadily upward, which is why you're here, today. We feel that more physical conditioning will improve their times."

She looped a strand of her shoulder-length blond hair behind her ear as she nodded earnestly. "Oh, definitely. Since your over-the-wall crew members are new to each other, it was tough to research them as well as I might have otherwise, but I did see that you have some strong guys…former football players, mostly. They have body mass, but I'm not so sure that they've had the sort of conditioning lately that would help keep a low center of balance. Would you happen to have a copy of the program that Mr. Mickowski has been following?"

Nathan glanced over at Perry, who shook his head. Nathan was pretty darned sure that was because Harley had never committed his workout program to paper. And if he had, it would have read "this week, spend a couple of hours in the gym."

"I'm sorry, we don't," Nathan said to their earnest interviewee.

"That's okay. I was curious, more than anything. I know that I would focus my program on increasing core strength and developing greater balance and agility. Working with such coordinated effort involves not only strength, but having the specific tasks imprinted on the proper muscle groups." She reached into her portfolio. "I have a few different training options mapped out. Nothing can be firm until I've personally assessed the crew, of course, but would you like to see my concepts?"

"That won't be necessary, Ms. Evans." Nathan's idea of a workout was his four-mile morning loop on the country roads around the headquarters. Whatever she had whipped up would be wasted on him.

Color climbed her throat and painted its way across her face. He'd rattled her again. For an instant he felt sorry for having done so, but if he gave her this job, she'd better get used to some flack. He was a nice guy compared to what she'd face in the way of resistance from the crew. If Perry and Harley weren't on board, her training would be taking place on one long, hard road. And judging by the stony expression still on Perry's face, he remained unconvinced. And Perry and Harley would be just the beginning of her problems.

The over-the-wall crew was growing restless, too. Some teams, who'd been together for a while, just flew in for races and then returned to their hometowns during the week. Because these guys had never worked to- gether as a unit, Harley had already required the non- residents to take temporary housing here, around Mooresville. All of them were itching to be back home.

Nathan could relate. His hunger to leave was nearly a living thing, the way it had begun to consume him. Usually, he did a decent job of containing his frustration, but facing this woman's sincere enthusiasm, he felt more an outsider than ever. He wanted to admire her—and grudgingly did—but more than that, he wanted to be done with this process and gone from this room. He looked across the table at Stacy Evans.

"You have no college degree. As I'm sure you know, that was a prerequisite for the job," he said.

She flinched almost as if he'd struck her. But again she quickly recovered. She gestured at her résumé, which sat before him.

"And I'm sure that you know that life experience is often as good as, if not better than, a piece of paper," she said. "Beyond that, you invited me here, fully aware that I don't have a degree. There must have been something about my qualifications that intrigued you, Mr. Cargill?"

He had no answer for that one, so he threw out a challenge of his own. "Tell me one solid reason you should have this position, and I don't want to hear about your passion for the sport or how you were born to do this job."

"I can reduce pit stop times by ten percent," she said flatly.

She'd barely hesitated. He was almost impressed, except she had to know that she'd just overpromised. He'd play her game, though, since she was otherwise the best candidate they'd seen. "That's half a measurement, Ms. Evans."

"Meaning?"

"Meaning it lacks the time period over which the improvement is to be achieved. I'll provide the other half. You have four weeks to get the job done. We're in Richmond this coming weekend, and I expect to see you here bright and early Tuesday morning."

Her blue eyes were wide with surprise and, if he didn't miss his guess, a little anger, too. Good, then. Anger would add to her drive.

"*Four* weeks?" she echoed.

"I believe I spoke clearly. You have a trial period of four weeks. If you attain the ten percent time drop, we'll discuss making this a permanent position." He wrote a figure on a slip of paper and slid it across the table to her. "That will be your weekly compensation during the trial period. I trust it's worth the risk?"

She glanced down, then nodded. "It's adequate."

What he'd written was more than adequate, and they both knew it. He stood before she'd even had a chance to gather up her papers and slide them back into the portfolio.

"Tuesday, then," he said. "If you'll follow me, I'll have my personal assistant get you through the required paperwork and background check."

Papers still only halfway away, she froze. "What sort of background check?"

"Criminal," he replied.

"Oh. Okay."

This time, she'd hesitated.

"Do you have a record?" he asked.

She laughed. "Oh, no, nothing like that," she said as she zipped shut her portfolio.

He'd wager that she was no criminal, but neither had

she been completely honest. Nathan wondered for a moment what she was hiding but decided that it didn't matter. She had already set herself up for failure. In four weeks, Kent Grosso's over-the-wall crew would be toned, and Stacy Evans would be gone. Now if he could only find a way to be gone, too.

CHAPTER TWO

As STACY BEGAN her pre-run stretching routine in the nearly empty Cargill-Grosso parking lot, she couldn't help but smile. Nathan Cargill had demanded her presence bright and early, hadn't he? She'd done Mr. Unapproachable one better and nearly beat the sun to work. She figured if she could get in a good run before facing her new clients, she'd leave some of her tension behind and be prepared to work.

She had a feeling that today was going to be less than stellar around the shop. Kent Grosso had finished thirty-second at Richmond. Stacy had no way of knowing how the over-the-wall crew had performed, but if it was as lackluster as Grosso's race, she'd be facing one ticked-off pack of guys. Not that they could be much worse than Cargill and Noble had been during her interview. That was for later, though…after the sun had fully lit the sky.

Though they were now into May, the early morning air held both the remainders of those April showers and a kiss of dew. It was a touch humid to be her favorite running weather, but at least she had the wonderful scent of the blooming magnolia trees lining the driveway to comfort her. On the driveway's edge sat a bench, likely for those waiting for their tour bus. For Stacy, it was the perfect brace to make sure her hamstrings were good and loose.

By her reckoning, she was nearly the luckiest woman in the world. She had no idea if she could actually pull off a ten percent drop in pit stop times over the next four weeks, but no one would fault her for lack of effort. This was her one chance, and not just for business success. That, she knew would come to her so long as she worked hard. But so far, hard work hadn't brought her into Kane Ledger's world, and this job would.

Kane was her half brother. He was also one of the sport's hottest agents, and his highest-profile client was none other than Kent Grosso. Kane was bound to show up at Cargill-Grosso, and Stacy was determined that this time he would acknowledge her. Granted, life with their mom, Brenda, had been awful. And granted, Kane, who was twelve years older, had left home when she was five. All the same he had been her bright spot…her hero. Now he wouldn't even take her calls.

Heaven knows she'd tried to reach Kane with the same head-on effort she put into everything. Once she'd realized that she was up against someone with a force of will as strong as hers, she'd accepted that she needed to find a new way to forge a connection with him. They'd had it once before, and she couldn't understand why he'd cut it off. She'd never done a thing to him, except love him. But that, too, was something to deal with later.

Stacy had just started down the driveway when she sensed someone behind her. She turned around and watched as Nathan Cargill came her way at a brisk walk. She wouldn't exactly call it an approach, since he was doing his best not to meet her eyes or acknowledge her presence.

Good luck with that.

"Good morning, Mr. Cargill," she called. "You're going to take a run, I see?"

She didn't know if the frown creasing his brow was a permanent affair, but she was beginning to think it just might be. He gave her a curt nod, but not a word.

"Well, I can tell you're going running because you surely wouldn't be dressed for office work like that," she said, doing her best not to get too wrapped up in the fact that he was muscled like a runner…lean and tall and strong.

Better to focus on the fact that the man seemed to think that stonewalling her was a new sport. Still he gave no response. But she'd dealt with deeper and more hurtful silences than what he could offer up and, despite his chilliness, she suspected she was going to like this man. Like her, he didn't back down. Nothing wrong with that!

"It's a fine morning for a run," she said. "Though, really, I try to start every day this way. Rain or shine, it doesn't matter, so long as I have time to sort my thoughts and get the proper outlook for the day."

He was even with her now, and she could better gauge his mood. *Mostly cloudy* pretty much covered it. She was tempted to get in a few more not-so-subtle nips at his silence, but something stopped her. Nathan Cargill had more than an underperforming team over which to be feeling out of sorts. Though it was none of her business at all—any more than her family situation should be his—Stacy was sure that he still had to be dealing with his father's death. Murder wasn't a quiet passing from old age, and an unsolved murder must be even more agonizing. She'd save her teasing for when she knew him better.

"I've always used my runs to help me sort through life," she said, keeping stride with his long gait when he obviously intended to pass her by. "I hope it brings you the same peace."

"Contrary to what you might have read or heard, I have no issues, Ms. Evans," he said in a voice that delivered images of snooty boarding schools and smug fraternity boys grown even more imperious with maturity.

That would teach her to be nice, she thought. Except she knew that was one lesson she really didn't want to learn. She *liked* being kind. Nobody had ever bothered much with her, which was all the more reason she wanted to send out some good stuff into the world.

"How nice for you," she replied, then took off jogging.

She'd save all her pent-up kindness for someone who deserved it and today, that clearly wasn't Nathan Cargill.

NATHAN LIKED rules. Rules gave structure, and structure provided the framework for success. And yet here it was not even seven in the morning and he'd already broken one of his cardinal employment rules: Treat employees as you'd like to be treated.

He'd been rude to Stacy Evans, but mornings were his time, six-thirty was his hour, and this road was *his* damn road. The last thing he wanted or needed was one short blonde in a shorter top and tight running pants to distract him. He picked up his pace from a brisk walk to a full jog and watched as she easily outdistanced him. It figured that the woman would run tall, too.

He hoped this exercise gave her the peace she was seeking because it was guaranteed that Harley Mickowski was going to be on her like a bad case of the flu the moment she entered the shop. He'd already warned Harley that Stacy Evans was not to be the target of team frustration—and they had plenty of that after Richmond—but then Nathan had just gone and done that very thing. He'd been raised to be more polite than that, and even discounting his upbringing, business compelled politeness.

No matter that he disliked sympathy in any form, much preferring to think that he was capable of handling what life had dealt him on his own. And no matter that he missed his father with an ache he could feel in his bones. He needed to put that aside and start with Ms. Evans as he would any new employee, distantly and yet politely.

Nathan picked up his pace to a steady run. As he followed her slender form down the road, watching her ponytail swing in rhythm to her easy gait, he decided that it wouldn't be such a bad thing to get along with a woman this well put together. Once she understood his rules and boundaries, it would all work itself out. Just then, she looked over her shoulder. Yes, she was still pretty, but far from soft. Based on the narrow set of her blue eyes, he'd judge her current, driving emotion to be annoyance.

He kicked out his stride a little longer. She glanced back again and then rolled into a full-out sprint. After a moment, she looked back again, and the meaning of her glare was clear: *Don't even try it.*

Nathan could catch her. At least, he was pretty certain he could. She looked to be darned quick and, while he'd never before literally chased down a woman in order to apologize, today he would. But then an image of hounds running down a fox in a hunt pushed through his mind, and he didn't like that one bit. He didn't much like the thought of trailing after her in perpetual second place, either. Since neither option was palatable, Nathan declared his morning run a total nonstarter. Frustrated, he turned back for headquarters. He'd share his road this one morning, but it wouldn't be happening again.

Forty-five minutes later, Nathan emerged from his office, showered, shaved and dressed for the day in his chosen corporate uniform of blue suit and a Harvard burgundy and crimson striped rep tie. One might be able to take the man out of Boston, but Boston would never be leaving the man. It wasn't as though his life in the Charlotte area was exactly barbaric. He'd been living in his father's sprawling ranch-style home in a local gated community—no hardship, but no great pleasure for a man accustomed to being in the thick of city life, either.

His office, which had been his father's before him, and which Dean Grosso had declined to take out of respect for both Alan and Nathan, was beyond comfortable. The Cargill racing team had been his father's passion and his life. Because he'd spent so much time at the office, he'd had a private bath, complete with shower and small sauna installed in his suite. The brown leather sofa that sat in the far corner of his office even pulled out into a bed for those frequent nights when his father had chosen not to leave at all.

Nathan had resented this industry when a child. He'd willingly gone to a boarding school for most of his youth just to avoid it. It wasn't until he was fully grown that he'd established a deeper relationship with his father. Then, he'd been through competing. He had simply built a world of his own. But over the past few months he had started to understand his father's love of NASCAR. And yet he was still a stranger in a strange land. The irony wasn't lost on him.

Nathan exited his suite and noted that Maria, his personal assistant, already sat at her desk. He greeted her and asked if there were any changes to the schedule he'd already pulled up on his computer screen before showering and dressing.

"None at all," she replied in a cool Boston accent that was so rare in these parts.

"Good enough," he said.

And that was the end of their conversation. She knew her boss well, knew when to work, knew when to socialize. Quite simply, they worked as an efficient team. When she'd agreed to his request that she come to Cargill-Grosso from his Boston business consultancy for this temporary assignment, he hadn't been surprised. It was exactly what he'd expected.

Nathan headed down to the far end of the hallway, where the building's main entry was located. The receptionist's desk was yet unoccupied, so that saved him another bit of small talk. He didn't have time for that, in any case.

Out in the shop, all was as he'd expected in Castillo's area. The engineers and mechanics were gathered around a workbench discussing the specs of a battery cover. Nathan moved on to the Grosso area. He knew Kent wouldn't be in. He had a list of appearances a yard long to satisfy this week. What he didn't expect, however, was to find the normally bustling areas out of public view to be empty as a wasteland. He half expected to see a tumbleweed roll across the shiny gray speckled finish on the concrete floor.

"Anyone?" he called.

No one answered.

Nathan moved on to the next bay, which led to the gym and the locker room. And there he found most of No. 414's team.

"Hal, what are you doing?" he asked the mechanic who stood, arms akimbo and legs set wide, guarding the locker-room door.

"Coach Stacy had to take a shower."

"And?"

"Someone's gotta guard the door," the man said, then broke into a wide grin. "It was my lucky day."

"And the rest of you?"

"Um…we're waiting to use the, ah, facilities."

"Good manners, Smitty," said Osbourne, the front tire changer, to the catch can man.

"How about you, Osbourne?"

The man shrugged his broad shoulders. "Just waiting to see if reality's as good as the rumors."

"Rumors?"

"She was running down the road when I pulled in. She's one heck of a knockout. She turned my head so far that I almost drove into one of those flowery trees," offered Stephens, the gas man.

"The tree's a magnolia," said Drew Lee, the rear tire changer and the only local on the over-the-wall crew. "They don't have those in Iowa?"

"Nah, not like here. We've got corn, though. A lifetime supply of corn, and more."

"I know something else you have, Stephens," Nathan said.

"What?"

"Work. Something you should be doing right now, and this isn't it. In fact, I'm betting that's true for all of you."

Nobody argued. They just drifted off to their regularly scheduled activities. Except Smitty, who had taken over guard duty in place of the mechanic.

"You can stand down," Nathan said.

"Stand down?"

He hitched his head in the direction the other men had taken. "You're relieved from guard duty."

"Aw, okay," Smitty said, then ever so slowly moved off.

Nathan had never seen the wiry man move at anything other than a fast clip. He couldn't say he blamed Smitty for stalling, but Nathan didn't much like the fact that he might have introduced another distraction to an already distracted team. At the very least, he had to find a workable morning routine for Cargill-Grosso's newest employee.

Standing at the post Smitty had vacated, Nathan

checked his watch, then shot a pointed look at the pit crew members who had already found an excuse to wander from their regular duties. Five minutes later, the locker-room door swung open, and Stacy Evans stepped out.

Her hair, the color of rich honey when wet, was again pulled into a ponytail. She wore no makeup, and her clothes were nothing more remarkable than a trim white T-shirt and a modest pair of dark blue exercise pants, but still there was something about her that captured a man's attention…his, included. And with a far greater degree than he cared to admit.

"Ms. Evans?" he said.

She adjusted the strap to the small duffel bag she had slung over her shoulder. "Why don't you call me Stacy?"

If he'd thought she was seeking comment to the offer, he would have told her that he liked the formal distance of calling her Ms. Evans. The bigger the wall between them, the better.

"I'd like to talk to you for a moment," he said instead.

She shrugged her slight shoulders. "Okay."

He looked at the team members now circling close enough to catch his conversation. "In the gym, if you don't mind."

"Sure," she said.

He led the way down to the end of the long shop building and the new gym annex, which his father had ordered built but not lived to see completed. When Nathan swung open the door, he wasn't especially surprised to find no one inside. The "if you build it, they will come" theory hadn't quite proved true with Harley calling the fitness shots.

"I hope the facilities will be sufficient," he said to Ms. Evans, who had gone to a low bench opposite the room's mirrored wall in order to set down her bag.

"Elliptical machines, free weights, treadmills," she murmured as she looked around the room. "The gym of my dreams. Now, what was it you wanted, Nathan?" Her mouth briefly quirked. "It is okay if I call you Nathan, isn't it?"

Since the rest of the employees did, he could find no reason to object…except for that distance he craved. "Nathan would be fine."

"Good," she replied, and her ponytail swung with her satisfied nod.

He closed the distance between them before speaking again. "First, I wanted to apologize for being abrupt with you this morning. It was wrong of me."

Nathan didn't know what she'd expected, but this clearly wasn't it. Stacy Evans was no poker face, and her surprise showed.

"Thank you," she said, once she'd recovered. "We all have our moments. Heaven knows I'm bound to have mine before I get this pit crew moving more smoothly."

This gave him the entrée to another topic he felt uncomfortable raising, necessary though it was. "Speaking of smoothly, I think it's going to be disruptive if you shower each morning down in the locker room."

She tilted her head, and her blue eyes narrowed marginally. "It's technically for both men and women, since you have no separate women's facility, isn't it?"

"Technically, yes."

"Then I can't see any reason for my not using the

shower. I need my morning run, and would prefer to take it here than before coming to work."

"I'm not suggesting that you skip your run, just that you not bring the entire garage to a standstill."

"What?"

"Most everyone felt the need to guard the door while you were in there."

A rosy pink began to paint her cheeks. "Oh. Well, I'm nothing so special once you get to know me. I'm sure in a few days I won't be interrupting the routine."

Nathan glanced to the opposite wall, where they were mirrored in their conversation. He couldn't believe that she didn't think herself special. In his experience, women this pretty had at least some self-awareness. She could be playing coy, but she didn't seem the type. Much as he preferred not to think in detail about their new fitness coach, he had to wonder what had blinded her to her own beauty. And he had to wonder why he was wondering...

"There's no point in waiting when you can use my private shower," he said. "We'll work out a schedule between the two of us."

"I wouldn't want to intrude."

"It's no trouble." At least, it was the most minimal trouble possible.

"If you're sure, then I'll accept your offer."

"Good."

"There's one more thing," she said. "When I came back from my morning run, I asked Harley Mickowski if he might be able to help me find some film of the over-the-wall crew to review. I also asked him if there was an office or a desk I could use, since there's nothing in here. He was, shall we say, less than helpful?"

Nathan could imagine. "We have the season's races to date on DVDs in the screening room, over in the administrative offices."

"I had thought as much. How do I reserve the room?"

"My assistant, Maria, will take care of it, and find a spot for you."

"Thank you. Then if you don't mind, I'll follow you over there," she said, slinging her bag back over her shoulder. "I'd like to get this done before I take up any of the crew's time."

"Of course," he said, and then went to open the door to the exercise room for her. It seemed that Stacy Evans hadn't been prepared for that politeness, though, since she reached for the door at the very same time, her hand closing over his.

"Sorry," she said, pulling her hand back as though she'd been shocked.

The feeling had been entirely mutual. He opened the door and stood to the side as she hurried through. Nathan didn't want to put a name to the electricity that had shot through him as her hand touched his. If he did, he'd be giving it more importance. And the more importance he gave that amazing jolt of sensation, the more pain/pleasure he was going to experience over the next four weeks, thinking of Ms. Evans showering just one thin wall away from him.

No trouble, he'd told her.

Make that no trouble for anyone but him.

CHAPTER THREE

STACY SAT in the dim light of Cargill-Grosso's small but elegant viewing room, waiting for Maria to arrive with the DVD of last weekend's race at Richmond. The smooth leather of her conference chair was cool beneath her admittedly hot palms. The primal excitement buzzing through her had nothing to do with focus, achievement, or overdelivery. She needed to get a grip, and quickly.

One touch of a man's hand shouldn't be enough to disrupt her concentration. And certainly one touch of a man's hand had never before been enough to make her heart race. But this time, touching Nathan Cargill had. She found it almost frightening.

Stacy had dated plenty, but never seriously. Work had to come first, and even if that hadn't been true, she knew that love was both fleeting and not to be trusted. That had been lesson number one learned at her mother's stiletto-shod feet.

Stacy knew her father's name and not much more. He'd been gone before she'd been out of a high chair. She'd never known or seen Kane's father at all. In fact, she'd never heard her mother mention him without then adding "may he rot forever in prison," as though it was some sort of ceremonial response.

Men had drifted through their ramshackle apartment in a haze of alcohol-fueled battles and cigarette smoke. Back when Kane had been there, he'd shielded her from the worst that had gone on. After he'd left, she'd done her best to protect herself. Still, though, she'd seen things that had left her with a dim view of love…or at least the kind of "poor helpless me" love that her once beautiful mother had specialized in.

But Stacy had escaped, she reminded herself. And if she could just focus, she'd be a step closer to entering her brother's world and getting him back into hers, as well.

The door to the viewing room opened with a subtle swish, and Maria entered. Maria was everything that Stacy knew she was not. Her dark hair was cut in the most current style, and her multicolored silk top and dark trousers were out of Stacy's mortgage-consumed budget range, for sure. Still, there was something open and friendly about the woman, who Stacy figured was near her own age.

"Here's the Richmond race," Maria said, setting a DVD in a plain slipcover on the dark walnut conference table. "Do you need any help with the equipment?"

"Probably," Stacy admitted. "I live a pretty low-tech life."

Maria went to a credenza that sat beneath the largest flat-screen television Stacy had ever encountered.

"It's pretty easy…just like home," she said.

Stacy laughed. "Home, in my case, has a television older than I am, and the cheapest DVD player I could find."

"Sounds like the temporary housing I'm renting," Maria said.

"Renting?"

Maria nodded as she slipped the DVD into the player. "Yes. I'm on temporary assignment with Nathan. When he heads back to Boston, I'll go, too."

"Any idea when that will be?" Stacy asked, wondering if it would be before her four-week trial period was up, then pushing aside the errant thought.

Why should she care when Nathan Cargill left? At this point, she'd be better off taking her chances with Perry Noble than with a man who made her feel as though she'd had *ditz* tattooed across her forehead.

Maria brought Stacy the remote. "Soon, I believe."

Try as she might to deny it, Stacy still felt an odd twinge of regret.

"Are you looking forward to leaving?" she asked Maria.

"I like it here, but, yes, I'll be ready to head home. I got engaged a month before coming to North Carolina, and I have to say that long-distance romance is tough."

"No doubt," Stacy said. Heck, in her book, any form of romance was tough. And pointless.

"But business is business, and that's what I keep reminding myself," Maria said briskly.

Good plan, Stacy thought. Business was business, and from now on, she would keep her emotions completely in check and out of the workplace.

"The buttons on the remote are pretty self-explanatory, so you should be all set," Maria said. "And just in case Nathan forgot to mention it this morning, welcome to Cargill-Grosso."

"He did forget that. You know your boss well."

"After six years together, I'd better. And I hope we get to know each other a little better, too."

Stacy smiled. It was nice to have one ally in the face of all the speculation and subtle hostility she'd encountered out in the shop.

"Have fun," Maria said as she left the room.

No problem there, Stacy thought as she started reviewing the Richmond pit stops, fast forwarding through Kent Grosso's already speedy circuits around the track.

Stacy didn't consider herself an especially girly girl, but while watching the orchestrated movements of the over-the-wall pit crew clearing the low, light-blue-and-white Smoothtone Music banner adorned pit divider wall, waiting for Kent to pull to a halt, then speedily jacking up the car, changing the tires, refueling and letting the car back down, she couldn't help but think of a testosterone-laden ballet. She grinned at the image, one she'd do better not to share with her new clients.

On a white notepad she'd earlier gotten from Maria, Stacy began to take notes. She already knew the names of her crew and had watched them in action before getting the job, so this time she was looking for fine detail.

The first man she reviewed was Drew Lee, whom she'd actually met before. Carrie, his wife, was one of her private clients and had told Stacy of this opening. Drew was a former college football star who'd finished business school before deciding that he wasn't yet ready for the suit and tie world, full-time. He worked as a rear tire changer for Kent Grosso and also worked with his father's business in Charlotte.

Though it was the last thing Drew would be willing to hear, he was beginning to get a little soft from office life. This, Stacy knew, would be an easy fix. Carrie was among the few clients she was still fitting into her evening schedule. In fact, she had an appointment with her at eight, tonight. A few competitive nudges from athletic Carrie would get Drew squarely in Stacy's new program.

The rest of the crew was more problematic. She didn't know them and had no quick route to motivate them into participation. NASCAR-wide, almost all members of over-the-wall pit crews were highly trained and specialized athletes. This was a far cry from the beginning days, when the mechanics had served as over-the-wall crew, too. But as the cars grew faster and the competition tighter, all jobs on a racing team had become more specialized. Now, the over-the-wall crew had to be the fastest of the fast, considering the intense surroundings in which they worked. Kent Grosso's pit crew was no different. Individually, their credentials and experience in both athletics and racing were awesome. Collectively, they had issues.

Three hours later, after countless run-throughs of the pit stops, Stacy felt somewhat closer to a solution. It wasn't as though there had been a colossal failure in the process at Richmond. There had, however, been hesitation and what appeared to be friction during the stops.

Muscles tight after sitting for so much longer than she was accustomed to, Stacy rose and stretched, then left the conference room for the small cubicle near the file room that Maria had cleared for her. An hour after that, she had written out eight exercise programs—seven for her over-the-wall crew and because it just might help her remember her true role around Nathan Cargill, one for him, too.

She pulled together her papers, then went to Nathan's office. Maria wasn't at her desk, so Stacy ventured on to Nathan's door, which was open. She peeked into the office, but no one was there. Stacy lingered in the doorway until the temptation to explore became too strong. It wasn't as though she wanted to riffle through the papers on Nathan's desk, but she did want a better sense of what he was about. All in the name of work, of course.

As she looked around the room, calm eased over her. The window blinds were turned just enough to keep the room bathed in ribbons of morning sunlight. With its antique desk and dark leather armchairs, the large room reminded her more of an exclusive men's club than an office. Against one wall was a sofa in the same mocha shade of leather as the pair of chairs in front of the desk. Above the sofa were framed photos.

Telling herself that a little more snooping would bring only the tiniest bit of tarnish to her karma, she moved closer. One photo was a fairly recent shot of Nathan with Kent Grosso and other members of the team. The most amazing aspect of the picture was that Nathan was truly, actually smiling. As she looked at his image, that same silly rush of excitement that she'd experienced when they'd touched zipped through her again. Her heart began to pound to a slow, sexy beat.

Step back. Wa-a-a-y back.

How could she be exhibiting the sort of fan-girl

behavior she'd last lavished on posters of her favorite pop stars when she'd been a kid? Nathan Cargill was a man, no better or worse than those in the shop toiling over engines and bodies, or those in any other walk of life. And he was her boss.

"Bad, scary, and wrong," she told herself.

She had to stop this. But maybe keeping Nathan at arm's length wasn't quite far enough. Stacy decided she needed to push him away as she had all males, from the long-ago moment she'd realized that she was blessed to be considered a jock. Back on Maria's desk she found a packet of yellow sticky notes. She quickly jotted a note. Then, before she lost her willpower, she left her exercise routine—and a snippy little challenge—on his chair. If these in-your-face tactics didn't drive away Nathan Cargill, nothing would.

LUNCH HAD COME and gone, unmarked by Nathan. With the race at Darlington quickly approaching, and a whole lot to be fixed after the ugliness that had been Richmond, this was going to be a bear of a week for Kent Grosso's whole team. The sole bright spot—and it had been a big one—was Roberto Castillo's eighth-place finish.

After Nathan's morning encounter with Stacy Evans, he had moved on to Dean Grosso's office. Dean was determined to be a hands-on owner, to the degree that his wife, Patsy, would tolerate after his years of being gone for races and a heavy-duty PR schedule. Today, they'd had hours of meetings with Kent, Perry, and the chief engineers and fabricators about everything that needed fine-tuning.

Then Dean had just wanted to shoot the breeze alone with Nathan, something few did since he'd fallen under suspicion in his father's murder investigation. And so they'd talked. Nathan appreciated Dean and Patsy's support, and he respected both of them enormously. Even more so now that they'd stood by him without a second thought.

Nathan tried not to take other people's suspicious looks and talk behind his back personally, except that it was so damned personal that anyone could think he would ever harm his father. He'd loved him, and just because he wasn't the sort to show emotion in public didn't make the feeling any less valid.

The best Nathan could do was neatly separate his life into work and family matters, and never let one bleed into the other. And the one man who could truly understand what he faced was Dean. With fresh rumors circulating about a daughter stolen from Dean and Patsy at birth, Dean had become adept at this sort of neat division, too. Nathan was learning much on that front from the older man. But now that he'd finally made it back to his office, all he wanted was peace.

"Want my protein bar?" Maria asked as he paused in front of her desk. "You look like you could use a boost."

He scrutinized the bar that she'd slid to his side of the desk. It looked nothing like the real meal he craved. "Thanks, but I'm not eating something that probably tastes like dog food."

"Didn't know you'd tried dog food," she said dryly.

Nathan had to smile in spite of his feeling that the world was lining up at his heels with the intention of running him down.

"Would you cancel all my appointments for the rest of the afternoon? I need some time to catch up with Liberty Partners," he said, referring to his Boston consultancy business. He was fighting hard to rebuild Liberty, which was also due for a renaming since Nathan no longer had a partner. He'd recently discovered that his partner had embezzled the company nearly dry. One more nasty bit of business that fate had thrown Nathan's way…

"Too late," Maria said. "You already have visitors. Sure you don't want the protein bar?"

Nathan took a quick look into his office. Harley and Perry occupied the two guest chairs, and Stacy sat on the couch, looking as though she'd been exiled to her own island.

Couldn't just one thing go smoothly today?

"Keep it for me," he said, then slid the bar back across to Maria. "Looks like I might need it after this."

"Guaranteed," Maria said.

And with that gloomy assessment ringing in his ears, Nathan entered the newest battleground.

"I take it we have an issue," Nathan said as he rounded to his side of his desk.

"You bet we do," said Harley. "That girl—"

Stacy stood. *"Girl?"*

Harley's satisfaction at getting under her skin spread across his face in a broad smile. "You are a girl, aren't you?"

"About as much as you're a boy," she replied.

"Hang on, you two. Let me get settled and then we'll talk," Nathan cut in. Scratch the protein bar. What he wanted was a vacation. "Maria, please bring in a chair from the conference room for Ms. Evans," he called to his assistant.

When he went to pull out his own chair, he noticed a sheet of paper on it. He picked it up and gave it what he planned to be a cursory glance. In neat and decidedly feminine handwriting was an exercise routine, the contents of which didn't interest him. What did, though, was the small, yellow square of paper attached to it, reading, *This might help you keep up, but somehow I doubt it.* His gaze shot to Ms. Evans, who hitched her chin a bit higher, when it had been hostilely positioned to begin with.

Interesting.

Nathan sat, then thanked Maria for wheeling in the chair. There was just enough room to fit it between the leather club chairs in which Perry and Harley sat.

"Why don't you join us, Ms. Evans?"

She did, somehow managing not to look at the men to either side of her. He'd been right when he'd pegged her as determined. Funny, but as much as he didn't want to think of her as other than an employee, he couldn't seem to keep her in that role.

Nathan focused on the only member in the trio who remained silent. "Perry, why don't you tell me what this is about?"

"Your new strength and conditioning coach has told the over-the-wall crew that they need to reaudition for their spots on Thursday."

The crew chief's response had been flatly delivered, much as Nathan had heard him speak when firing those who broke the team's rules.

"And how do you feel about this?" Nathan asked,

figuring they were better off getting the emotion—such as it was, in Perry's case—out of the way.

"It's insane," the older man replied in the same level voice. This was the reason he'd made it to where he had as a crew chief. With Perry, it wasn't so much grace under pressure as never seeming under pressure.

"Insane? Insane doesn't begin to say it!" Harley cried.

"This is ultimately Perry's area and Perry's analysis," Nathan said.

Harley went on, unchecked. "If Dean hears about this garbage, he'll—"

"Enough," Nathan said in a louder voice. "Ms. Evans is my responsibility, and Dean has already given his approval to her hiring and whatever course of action she chooses to take."

"He'd take it back if he knew what was going on," Harley said, color now suffusing his beefy face.

"Ms. Evans—" Nathan began.

"Stacy. I want to be called Stacy."

It didn't seem like good timing on her part to be arguing this issue, but if he called her Stacy, at least she'd leave the office having won one small point.

"Okay, Stacy, then," Nathan said. "Would you explain your reasons for having the crew reaudition?" Not that he could come up with any good reasons to effectively undo what had been done months before.

"There are three," she said with a calmness that competed with Perry's.

For her sake, Nathan was glad she'd cooled down. If she waged a war of escalation with Harley, she'd flat-out lose. Her best route was around his objections, and he was pleased to see that she was sharp enough to figure this out. She appeared to have good instincts. He liked that about her.

"The first reason is that among your tire changers and tire carriers, you have men who've done both jobs at one time or another. You've let them choose slots based on preference, which is good for morale, but maybe not what they're best suited for, physically."

"Okay," Nathan said. "And that would be Perry's decision after consulting with Harley. Next reason?"

"After watching the pit stops in Richmond and talking to the guys, I get the feeling that they haven't gelled as a team. If they each try out for all positions, they'll have a better idea of what the other is doing. It's about unity and understanding."

"Is this the part where we all hold hands and sing 'Kum Ba Yah'?" Harley asked.

"It might help your negative outlook," Stacy said in a cheery voice.

Nathan fought hard to hide a smile.

"Go on," he said to her.

"Finally, before I can get the crew to really achieve, they have to buy into the concept of individual reinvention. They need to let go of some old thoughts and know that their bodies can do even more than they now believe. What better way than to let, say, the catch can man give it a real and meaningful try as a tire carrier?"

"And who will decide if there are job changes among the crew?" Nathan asked.

"Perry, with Harley's input, of course. I'm nowhere near qualified to do that," Stacy said. "But, really, this is a lot more about what the guys learn on the way than it is expecting any change in roles."

A very diplomatic answer, from Nathan's point of view, but still one that presented another problem, one he wasn't sure she could even recognize.

"But by not really expecting any job changes, aren't you risking something else? How do you think the crew would feel if they found out you were toying with them?" he asked.

"But I'm not. I'd never do that to another person. And of course I've thought about this. That's why I need buy-in from Perry and Harley."

She turned her attention to Perry. "If you see a change that needs to be made, by all means, make it. This is your crew and your call. I'm just trying to find a way to make them work together on all levels."

"So, what do you think now, Perry?" Nathan asked the crew chief, growing even more impressed with Stacy's ability to hold her own in a business battle.

Noble's answer was almost instantaneous. Like a lot of men in his field, he went by instinct when in a tough spot. "It sounds like a mix of spiritual and corporate voodoo, but so long as everyone in this room is clear that I still choose and run the over-the-wall pit crew, I'll let her have a shot at it."

Nathan glanced at Stacy. She didn't look especially relieved.

"How about you, Harley?" she asked the pit crew coach.

"You're gonna step on a lot of toes while you're here, aren't you?"

She smiled. "Probably, but I'll try to do it as gently as possible."

He shook his head. "I'm not giving you buy-in, or

whatever fancy phrase you want to stick on it, but I will keep out of your way…this week, at least."

Nathan leaned back in his chair and looked at the trio assembled before him. "I'm glad you worked this out, because otherwise, gentlemen, I was going to have to force this idea down your throats."

"It surely goes better with a spoonful of sugar, doesn't it?" Stacy said.

Perry snorted. "I'm not mistaking either you or Nathan for Mary Poppins. You've got your week, now make it work." He stood and left the office, with Harley lumbering after him.

After they had left, Nathan watched as the stress eased from Stacy's features.

"Thank you," she said.

"For what?"

"For supporting me."

"If I hadn't believed in the idea, I wouldn't have. But, generally, good acts and ideas get support, don't you think?"

She smiled, but with more sorrow than humor in her eyes.

"Not so much in my experience," she said.

He knew that her sadness shouldn't affect him on such a personal level. He shouldn't want to know where it came from, or why…but he did. Still, he wouldn't pry.

"Really? I'm sorry to hear that," he said.

"Don't be. I'm sure my journey has made me a better person, even if I haven't always especially liked the path," she replied, then stood. "I suspect that beneath that smooth exterior, you're a very nice man, Nathan

Cargill. Now I just need to figure out if that's good news or bad to me."

And long after she left, Nathan tried to decide the very same thing about Stacy Evans.

CHAPTER FOUR

"HOME."

As Stacy pulled into the parking spot in front of her town house, she said the word one more time just for the sound of it. Until she'd bought this place, as modest as it was, she'd never had anything that was just hers. She couldn't have been any prouder if she'd built it brick by brick, herself.

It was now a quarter past ten at night, and she was bone-tired, both from her day at Cargill-Grosso and from her training session with Carrie Lee. She and Carrie had run together, gone through Carrie's post-baby abdominal exercises, and then finished up with a short yoga session. And tomorrow Stacy would rise at six and start her whole work-till-you drop routine again, except that it would be her night to be the student, since she had her weekly Anusara yoga classes on Wednesdays.

Because there was no way but forward in all of life, she jogged the rise of five concrete steps to her town house's entry after waving at Mrs. Lorenzo, her widowed elderly next door neighbor, who kept watch from her front window each night as Stacy arrived home. Stacy suspected that Mrs. Lorenzo's attentiveness had sprung from having an ear and eye for gossip. When she'd found that Stacy's life was plain as vanilla pudding, she'd kept watching, though. Stacy got a kick out of the older woman, her changing array of hair colors, and what she called her "gentlemen callers." Mrs. L was quite the hit down at the Senior Center. If Stacy ever found the time to date again, she just might take tips from her neighbor.

For now, though, she had her own little family to keep her company. She unlocked her front door, stepped inside and relocked the door, then set her gym bag by the entry closet that contained her apartment-size washer and dryer.

"I'm home," she called, though she knew odds on getting an answer were slim to none.

Stacy switched on the light to her living room, which was furnished in what she liked to call Salvo Swank. She'd found most of her furnishings at a local Salvation Army store, and was quite thankful that the wealthier in Charlotte seemed to frequently upgrade their furniture. She'd made herself a warm and welcoming home on a pauper's budget, which was all she'd had left after taking the leap into home ownership.

"Hello, Hazel," she said to the goldfish in its spacious tank.

Then she moved on to Beau, her senior citizen of a hamster, who didn't seem to know that he was setting a record for longevity. Unlike Hazel, who was actually more like Hazel the Fourteenth. What Stacy lacked in human family, she'd done her best to make up for with the animal kingdom. She'd known that while doing it, which she supposed would save her from being one of those scary newspaper stories about a woman living with three hundred cats. Well, self-awareness and an allergy to cats.

After feeding Beau and Hazel, she pampered herself with a long shower followed by her favorite snack of popcorn topped with sea salt and pepper. And just because she deserved it, she added a minuscule amount of melted butter to the mix. Content down to her bones, Stacy moved on to her tiny guest-room/office and settled in front of her one indulgence—her computer. While she didn't need jewels or a car any fancier than Maude, she did crave knowledge, and a world's worth of it waited at her fingertips, courtesy of her computer.

Stacy's ritual was the same every night. She'd catch up on her e-mails from clients and friends—who were often one and the same people—and then she'd pick her topic for the night and see what she might learn. Recently, she'd been traveling the great cities of Europe without ever having to leave her home. Tonight, though, she was too tired to even cyber-trek. Instead, she went to her favorite search engine and typed in a name: Nathan Cargill.

The results that came back were nothing new to Stacy. As a NASCAR fan, she'd been as shocked as all others to read of Alan Cargill's murder at the annual celebration dinner in New York City. This time, though, reading about Nathan's presence there, and then seeing him termed a "person of interest" in his father's death hit far closer to her heart than to her curiosity.

Stacy wasn't naive or foolish. She knew that men of bad character could appear saintlike to the rest of the world. She also knew that greed could poison. Alan

Cargill had been a very, very rich man who many—including his own son—might have envied. She did, however, trust her instincts.

Nathan had his flaws, but beneath that unapproachable exterior, she believed he was too caring, too keyed into integrity, to ever commit an act that violated everything he stood for. And as for the possibility that it had been a crime of passion, she knew she'd do best by seldom putting the words *Nathan* and *passion* too closely together. They led down a different pathway, one she would not be taking.

But just as she'd allowed herself that little taste of butter, now Stacy closed her eyes and relived the sensation of feeling his skin against hers. One touch. One simple, accidental touch, and her world had changed. Crimes of passion she would never condone, but acts of passion she now understood. And in accepting this, she'd rattled herself much more than one sexy, enigmatic man could. Because tonight, she'd realized that she might have something in common with her mother, and that was never good. Tonight, even when safe in the home she'd made for herself, with the company of her little makeshift family, Stacy felt hungry for more. And if this craving was what had driven Brenda, Stacy would never, ever go there, because she was still her mother's daughter, and there might be no turning back.

LIFE, NATHAN KNEW, was a one-day-at-a-time proposition. The changes that had barreled at him over the past six months had been sufficient to drive that point home. Based on that one day scale of measurement, today had been a success.

Never mind that it was nearly midnight and the closest he'd come to relaxing was shedding his suit jacket and tie and leaving his shoes at the door when he'd gotten home. Not that this place was exactly home. It had been his father's home, purchased after Nathan left for college. It bore no trace of his youth and no memories but the occasional chat with his father before dinner at the local country club.

In calling the day a success, Nathan would also forget the fact that he'd left the office later than usual and had been surprised to see a rusty little car still in the employee parking area. No one with employment remotely related to cars would be caught dead driving that, so he knew it had to belong to Stacy Evans. Cargill-Grosso was certainly going to get its money's worth out of her. That, too, had been exactly what he'd expected. What he hadn't expected was that she'd be occupying his thoughts this late into the night.

Distracted, Nathan walked to the crystal decanter and tumblers that sat on the antique sideboard in his father's library. Because he needed something to take the edge off his energy, he poured himself a small shot of single malt Scotch. He absently wondered how his favorite liquor had ended up in the decanter. He supposed that the housekeeper had asked his dad for a list of Nathan's preferences before he'd taken up residence.

Lately he felt as though others were living the good parts of his life for him, while he went around untangling one mess after another. In ways, he found that theory a lot more palatable than admitting that *this*— the constant speculation about him, a home that wasn't a home, the temporary workmates, the troubled business back in Boston—was what his life truly had become.

Nathan raised his glass to himself and said, "No point to a postmortem."

Instead, he went to the computer that sat in the library's nook and began to sort through his personal e-mail. He found one from Jennifer, the investment banker he'd been casually dating back in Boston. Usually, her sharp wit and sharper cracks about how he must be suffering while south of the Mason-Dixon Line amused Nathan. Tonight, though, he found her comments a little too tinged with snobbery. All in all, he'd preferred Stacy's gentler humor today. After writing Jennifer a brief "doing fine…no idea when I'll be back" reply, he didn't give her another thought.

Nathan skipped over the alumni e-newsletters, the spam that had escaped his e-mail program's filter, and even an e-mail from his father's attorneys, since he knew nothing further would be happening with probating his father's estate until Nathan was officially declared no longer a suspect in the murder. Below that, though, was an e-mail from Overstreet Investigations.

Nathan had hired Hank Overstreet the instant he'd realized that Lucas Haines, the NYPD detective assigned to his father's case, clearly considered him a prime suspect, even if he'd never been that direct in his statements to the media. Haines was, in Nathan's experience, both smart and determined. Normally, this would make him someone Nathan would like. For Haines, he'd make an exception.

Nathan was sick of being treated like a liar and a

criminal. He had told the truth when interviewed at the hotel and he'd never wavered from that truth. He had nothing to do with his father's death. Yes, he had been gone from the ballroom at the approximate time his father had been fighting for his life, but he hadn't been alone. He'd been with Mallory Dalton almost the entire time. And for those few minutes she'd been in the ladies' room, he'd chatted with a waitress. He couldn't help it if the waitress had left her job and couldn't be traced. It looked ugly, but he wasn't lying.

Overstreet's e-mail was entitled Update. Nathan knew the news was nothing good, or Hank would have called him. And as he read, his concerns were affirmed. The server's name, Maya Rodriguez, had been as false as the social security number she'd provided the hotel. Overstreet said that odds were good the young woman was an illegal alien or otherwise on the run, which would make it difficult to trace her. If Nathan would authorize the funds, Hank wanted to do a series of follow-up interviews in New York City.

Nathan sent off a quick confirmation. Between the embezzlement at Liberty Partners and the added expense of retaining Overstreet, he was as close to broke as he'd ever been in his life. This, though, was money he couldn't afford not to spend. Between being broke and facing a murder trial, he'd take broke any day of the week.

He was well aware, too, that his concept of broke probably sat in a different place on the scale than that of someone like Stacy Evans. He'd grown up with every advantage, and never would he complain about where he'd landed in life. This was his battle, and damned if

Nathan would lose it, any more than he could ever imagine Stacy backing down.

Even now, hours later, as he thought of the fire that had flashed in her eyes when Harley had called her a girl, he had to grin. Maybe he and Stacy had more in common than he'd first believed. And if not, he could have a darned good time while finding that out. Maybe he needed to begin to live *all* of his life again. He could start that with Stacy Evans.

"THE DEAL IS THIS," Stacy said to her over-the-wall crew early on Wednesday morning. "I'm never going to have you do something I wouldn't be willing to do."

She stared at the faces of each of her men, all of whom were looking a little put out to be in running clothes and on display for the tourists already pulling down Cargill-Grosso's driveway, in search of a NASCAR star sighting.

Calvin Glass, the front tire carrier, snorted. "Right. I don't see you reauditioning for your job like we're going to tomorrow."

Calvin probably had less to worry about than anyone gathered under that magnolia tree. He was both an engineer and an Olympic-level track and field athlete who'd also taken a job in Cargill-Grosso's design department when he'd joined the team. He was as close to an insider as one could be. All the same, she could see that he was hiding worry, something she was a pro at doing, too.

Though "honesty is the best policy" wasn't an adage that her mother had bandied about very much, it was one that Stacy had learned well from both her brother,

Kane, and from other role models who'd come after him. And so she decided that these guys deserved her honesty.

"Then I'll let you in on a little secret," she said. "I'm auditioning for my job right now. I have four weeks to get a ten percent time drop out of all of you, or I'm out of here."

"No way," said Osbourne. "No way would you agree to that."

"Let's just say that Nathan Cargill caught me in a weak moment."

Osbourne grinned. "He's good at that, so I guess you're not feeding us bull."

"I've got no reason to lie. In fact, by telling you, I've let you guys know just how much power you have over my fate." She paused for what she hoped was comedic effect. "Now, the question is, are you going to use it for good or for evil?"

A couple of the guys laughed, and Stacy began to relax.

"Now, back to business," she announced. "As I said, I'm not going to make you do something I'm unwilling to do, and so right now, all of us are taking a run. Nothing big. Just a couple of miles."

"Miles?" muttered Drew Lee. "Carrie made me run before work."

Last night, Stacy and Carrie had joked about Carrie's planned incentive approach to improved fitness. Suffice it to say that Drew hadn't suffered when given his sweet reward.

"Come on, Drew. It'll go by faster than you think," Stacy said. "So let's go do it!" She started down the driveway, hoping that the guys' competitive natures would soon stifle their grumbling. She didn't look back, though, because that would be admitting she had doubts about her ability to lead. That was one little secret she'd be keeping to herself.

It wasn't too long before she heard the footfalls of the men behind her.

Calvin easily cruised by and said, "You might want to pick up the pace, Coach."

Stacy laughed. "You just keep going until you're tired or in the next county, okay?"

As the rest of the crew laughed, Stacy felt her day brighten. One run as a team wasn't going to guarantee that she'd achieve her goal, but it sure moved her one giant step closer.

They were about a half mile out on the winding country road when an expensive-looking black sports car passed them heading in the opposite direction, then came to a quick halt. Stacy looked over her shoulder to see the car backing up. She stopped, turned, and shielded the sun from her eyes with one hand. The car stopped again when it had pulled even to her, and the driver's window came down.

"Good morning," Nathan said.

At least this time she had the excuse of a little exercise for her increased pulse.

"Good morning," she said in return.

"I just came from a meeting with Dean Grosso."

She wasn't sure what she was supposed to say to that, but Nathan looked as though he was having trouble finding his words, too. Who'd have figured?

"I hope the meeting went well," she finally said.

He gave a distracted nod. "Fine…great."

Stacy noticed that her guys were now jogging in place in a semicircle around them, and they looked far too entertained for her comfort.

"Keep on moving. I'll catch up," she said to them.

"So, before I take off, was there something you wanted to say?" she asked Nathan.

Again, he hesitated, and Stacy followed his line of vision. The guys had kept on moving, but at the pace of sleepy turtles.

"This looks like bad timing," Nathan said. "Can you meet me in my office around eleven? I should be between meetings."

"Sure," she said with all the calm she could muster. Inside, she could feel Neurotic Stacy fighting to get out and ask, "This isn't about anything bad, is it? I'm not about to be fired before I was even hired, am I?" But early on she'd learned that life went better when she kept Neurotic Stacy under lock and key.

Nathan said. "I'll see you then."

But how, exactly, she'd last until eleven was something Stacy contemplated during the rest of her run.

At ten of eleven, Stacy stood outside Nathan's office making small talk with Maria. Or at least trying to make small talk. When Maria had to take a phone call, Stacy wasn't sure who was more relived to have an out—she or Maria.

Just a few minutes before eleven, a couple of men in suits walked out of Nathan's office, and he called her in.

"Sit down," he offered, gesturing at one of the fat leather chairs.

Stacy sat and waited for Nathan to begin. Instead of launching into an explanation of why she had to pack her things and leave, he said, "Lawyers."

"Pardon me?"

"The men who just left…lawyers. They give me a headache," he said, while riffling through his desk drawer. "Sometimes I think that the paperwork regarding my dad's businesses will never end. Dad had given me power of attorney, so now I'm doing all of the late signing on his behalf." He pulled out an aspirin bottle, uncapped it and shook two loose. "So, the reason I asked you here was to tell you that Dean and Patsy are having a dinner at the farm tomorrow, and I wanted to know if you'd like to come along?"

Stacy had heard about the big dinners at Villa Grosso, more commonly known as "the farm." Never, in a million years, had she expected to be invited to one.

"With you?" she blurted.

He popped the aspirin into his mouth, then took a swallow from a bottle of spring water that sat on the right-hand edge of his desk blotter.

"That would be the general idea," he said once the aspirin were down.

Like a date? "But I wasn't invited."

"Yes, you were, by me…just now. And if it makes you feel any better, I cleared it with Dean this morning."

"But Patsy doesn't know?"

"She'll be fine with it. The bigger the crowd, the better, at these prerace dinners, as far as she's concerned. You'll see a lot of folks from Cargill-Grosso and a lot of industry people."

"Industry people?"

"Agents, sponsors…"

"Agents?"

He smiled. "Yes, agents. Am I not making sense? You keep repeating me."

"Sorry. I'm just a little distracted." *By the whole date concept. And the thought that if I do go, Kane might be there.*

Nathan recapped the aspirin bottle and put it back into his desk. "I figured this would be a good chance for you to get to know more people in the organization. You can very seldom find everyone under one roof."

So, not a date. Stacy knew she should feel relieved, but she just didn't seem to be able to do it. On some crazy level, she wanted a date with him.

"So are you interested?" Nathan asked.

"I am. Thank you very much for thinking of me."

He glanced down at some papers on his desk and said something under his breath that for all the world sounded to Stacy like, "You don't know the half if it."

"Pardon me?" she asked.

"Nothing, just having a lawyer flashback," he said. "If you're feeling uncomfortable about the late invitation, look at tomorrow as part of your job. The closer our organization is, the better we'll run."

Clearly, he hadn't been thinking of *close* in quite the same manner that had been popping into her mind. All for the better, Stacy supposed.

"The dinner begins at six-thirty," Nathan said. "We'll leave right from work at six-fifteen, if that's okay by you?"

"That should work out perfectly. Perry, Harley and I should be through reauditioning the guys well before that," Stacy replied. "Should I bring anything?"

"Nothing but your appetite."

Her appetite and a whole lot of prayers that Kane would be there, that she wouldn't make a fool of herself if he was, and that very, very soon, she'd get over this insane crush on Nathan Cargill.

All things considered, she'd rather have been bringing potato salad.

CHAPTER FIVE

A GOOD NIGHT'S SLEEP would have been very helpful, Stacy admitted to herself as she stood under the invigoratingly sharp spray of the shower in Nathan's office suite. Even a bad night's sleep would have been a leg up over what she'd managed, but that hadn't been part of her overactive brain's agenda. By six, she'd been running the same route she'd taken with the guys yesterday, except this time it had been a solitary effort. It had worked, too. Though she was sure she'd crash and burn of exhaustion around eight tonight, right now she felt serene.

After pulling on her warm-ups and T-shirt and combing her hair back into a ponytail, she took a few minutes to make sure that she'd left the shower and vanity top tidy. Nathan was walking into the office at the exact time she was closing the bathroom door behind her. Both of them jumped, and Stacy squeaked pretty much like a scared mouse on helium. Not one of her better sounds…or moments.

"Sorry, I was just finishing up my shower," she said in a rush. "I figured that since you told me it would be okay to use your bath, and…"

He was looking at her oddly. Because she felt more

comfortable pinning an interpretation on an act than just letting it float out there in Unexplainable Land, she decided that he didn't like the way she looked. "Don't worry. I brought something else to wear to the farm tonight."

He still stood in the doorway, appearing, for lack of a better word, dumbfounded.

"A dress. I brought a dress."

The way he was looking at her, she might as well have been speaking in tongues.

"Hey, can I get you some coffee or something?" she asked.

He seemed to shake himself out of whatever had gripped him. "Thanks, no. I can get my own." With that, he turned and left.

"Okeydoke," Stacy said to herself and then headed back to the gym to wait for her guys. She'd chalk up that exchange with Nathan as an intro to whatever weirdness she got from the over-the-wall pit crew as they reauditioned. She doubted they could pull anything stranger than Nathan had.

When she opened the gym door, Stacy immediately reassessed her team's willingness to be weird. It wasn't even seven-thirty, yet all eight men were standing shoulder to shoulder, with their hands behind their backs, waiting for her. Calvin stepped forward.

"Last night, when we got together for a few refreshments after work, we decided that today was as good a time as any to see if you're a woman of your word."

"Any word in particular?" Stacy asked.

"That talk about not having us do anything you wouldn't do," he said.

Osbourne and Smitty stepped forward. Each brought forward an item they'd been hiding behind their backs. One was a helmet, and the other a uniform in the Smoothtone Music colors.

Stacy nodded. "Ah, I see. You want me out there trying your jobs, too."

"Exactly," Calvin said.

"And this is the part where you think I'll go all girly and back down?"

"Could be," Calvin replied.

"Think again." Stacy walked to Osbourne and collected the uniform. Then Smitty handed her the helmet.

"Good enough," Calvin said. "See you at the pit box in half an hour."

The team turned with military precision and headed for the door.

"I told 'em you wouldn't back down," Drew Lee said out of the side of his mouth as he passed by.

Back down? Heck, she was downright excited!

HELMET IN HAND and uniform on, Stacy made her way to the practice pit box located on the hardtop behind the garages, hidden from tourists and, she hoped, anyone else in the mood for a little amusement. The pit box was similar to one you would find at a NASCAR track, complete with the yellow markings on the ground and the low banner-covered barrier that served as the pit wall.

In a race, so long as the car required only refueling, a tire change, or minor repairs, it would be serviced between the yellow marks. Anything more complex, or a car leaking fluid, had to be serviced behind the wall.

Though time was of the essence in those situations, too, the pit stop wasn't the same orchestrated affair, and didn't concern Stacy in her promised time reduction.

Because there was no point in taking up the time and attention of anyone other than her over-the-wall pit crew, the support crew, Harley and Perry, for the purposes of this exercise, they were simply leaving a No. 414 chassis, without engine, parked between the yellow lines. Stacy wished for the excitement of watching the car come in and the dance begin, but it wouldn't have been practical.

"Ready for this?" Osbourne asked.

"Sure."

He hitched his thumb back over his shoulder. "The rest of the guys should be here in a minute. What job do you want to try first?"

"Eighth man," she said, and Osbourne laughed.

The eighth man was allowed over the wall only during the second half of the race. He cleaned the windshield, gave the driver water, and in certain situations, was allowed to add a glare shield to the windshield. Stacy figured she could handle that. Of course, real eighth men also held another job of some sort with the racing team. And on top of that, they had to have all the other over-the-wall jobs down pat, in case of injury or illness of a pit crew member. But Stacy wasn't too worried about being "real" today.

"How about you shoot a little higher and try tire carrier?" Osbourne suggested.

"Can't wait to see that," said Calvin, who'd just joined them.

Steve Markoff, the rear tire carrier, nodded in agreement. "It's not as easy as we make it look, you know?"

"I'm pretty sure of that."

The rest of the team had arrived, as had Harley and Perry.

"What's this about?" Harley asked, gesturing at her team garb.

"I'm walking a mile in the guys' shoes today," Stacy said.

"We'd better see you running," said Drew, then gave her a wide grin.

"Crazy as the day is long," Harley muttered. "But go ahead and make a fool of yourself."

"Probably," Stacy agreed. "But I'm bound to learn something in the process."

"Take front tire carrier and I'll coach you," Calvin said. "And I'll make sure the crew takes it nice and slow for you."

"Okay." Stacy put on her helmet. Already her heart was beginning to pound. She figured it took a bit of an adrenaline lover to do this job, so she should be fine.

"Okay, on go," Calvin directed the guys. "Three, two, one…go!"

Stacy tried to take in what was happening around her, but even at their "nice and slow" pace, she was falling behind. Pryor, the jackman, already had the far side of the car up, and she was still trying to get the first tire out and around to the far side. She was extremely fit, but eighty pounds had never felt this heavy!

"That's it," Calvin yelled. "Now roll it."

Osbourne, the front tire changer, added in his two bits. "Ready when you are, Coach. Been ready for a while."

Stacy got the tire to him, and after she totally messed up getting it on the studs, he gave her a hand.

"Thanks," she muttered.

She grabbed the old tire and rolled it back to the wall, then got the nearside tire, which the support crew had delivered to her. At least this one hadn't been such a haul. Of course, Pryor had had the near side of the car jacked up for what seemed like forever, and Osbourne was waiting for her again. She was willing to bet that the gas man and the catch can man had finished their mock refueling and now were bored to death and discussing what they wanted to eat for lunch.

This time, Stacy got the tire straight onto the studs. Osbourne had the lug nuts tightened before she could even get the old tire back to the pit wall.

"Get the grille!" Calvin called.

"What?" In her frazzled state, all she could think was that the gas man and catch can man had decided to grill out.

"You need to check the car's front grille for debris," Calvin repeated.

"Oh." She hustled up and looked for imaginary debris. Finding none, she returned to the wall.

Pryor lowered the car, which would be the signal to Kent that the pit stop was complete. And awful. She pulled off her helmet as the guys gave her a round of applause.

"No, really," she said, then gave them her best humble grin. "I guess I just proved the old adage of those who can't do, teach."

"You didn't look too bad for a rookie," she heard another voice comment. And not a voice from the pit crew, either. Just then, she noticed Nathan, and wondered how much of her clown act he'd witnessed.

"She didn't look 'too bad'?" Calvin said. "Bet you couldn't do much better."

"Tell you what, next week I'll take you up on that challenge."

Calvin chuckled. "You're just hoping I'll forget by next week."

Stacy decided she wasn't in the mood for this half-joking macho show. While she had to admit to being pleased over the look of admiration on her boss's face, she wanted him gone so that the blush she felt flaming across her own features could fade.

"But right now, we need to get down to business," she said to her guys. "Because we all want to go home sometime before midnight, and because I am admittedly without a single ounce of know-how, how about we say that I began and ended my over-the-wall experience with the job of front tire carrier?"

That was one thing the whole team agreed upon. Stacy and the guys soon came up with a rotation through positions so that everyone could be observed once. They had just finished the first mock pit stop when out of the corner of her eye, Stacy caught Nathan taking a call on his cell phone and then slipping away.

"Amen to that," she murmured under her breath. So far today, he'd seen her wet and ratty and dry and clumsy. She could only hope to the heavens that tonight he'd see her as the true professional she knew she could be. She told herself that she needed the validation for business reasons, but knew that as the fib it was. Foolish, she wanted Nathan Cargill to like her as much as she was already growing to like him.

Stacy Evans was timely, Nathan noted when she arrived at his office precisely at the agreed-upon time of six-fifteen.

"Better?" she asked.

"Better than what?"

Clearly, they'd had some sort of speech disconnect going on all day, and Nathan knew it was his fault. He couldn't say to her what he wanted to, not without making her uncomfortable, and so he was finding it tough to say anything at all.

"My dress," she said, smoothing her hands down flowery fabric that made him think of picnics, sunshine and laughter. "Do I look better than this morning?"

How could she even think that she'd looked bad this morning? Maybe she needed a close approximation of his truth, no matter how uncomfortable it made her.

"But you looked beautiful this morning," he said.

"Beautiful? Ha! I didn't have the slightest bit of makeup on and I was still wet from the shower."

"As I said, beautiful." She wasn't ready for the full truth of what he'd thought when he'd seen her—that he'd like that intimate sight again, but in his own home, after having spent the night making love to her.

"Well, though I think you sorely need your eyes checked, I'll say thank you."

Nathan laughed, something he found himself doing with increasing frequency when around Stacy.

"There's not a thing wrong with my eyesight," he promised. "Ready to go meet the rest of the Cargill-Grosso team?"

"As ready as I'll ever be," she said, settling her hand over the strap to her shoulder bag, or whatever the tiny red purse she carried was called. Nathan just knew he'd never had a date carry a purse that small. Not that Stacy Evans was his date, technically speaking.

"Then let's go." He ushered her out of his office, then down to his car. Because he was a gentleman, whether or not this was a date, he opened her car door for her.

"Jazzy," she said, looking down at the charcoal-gray leather seats. She slipped her purse from over her shoulder, then slid into the car. Nathan closed her door and went around to his side of the convertible.

"Top up or down?" he asked before starting the car.

"Oh, down!"

Her excitement touched him. It was almost as if she'd never been in a convertible before. Most of the women he'd dated had been much more jaded and not wanted to risk their hairstyle to the wind. Nathan released the top latch on his side of the car and then reached over and got the one in front of Stacy. They were close enough in the two-seater, and this brought them even closer. He could smell a hint of perfume, an uncomplicated floral scent that suited her sunny disposition.

He shifted back into his seat and reached for the button on the console that started the top down. As it settled in, he glanced at Stacy, who was pulling her hair back into its workday ponytail.

"Ready," she said when she was done.

The Grosso farm was just outside Mooresville, so Nathan took the drive slowly, and not just because he didn't want to arrive early. He was far more focused on having some time with just Stacy. He looked over at her again, and caught her regarding him intently. Instead of retreating from the moment, he decided to turn it into something else.

"How did the reauditions go?" he asked over the rush of the wind.

"Good, I think. Perry and Harley are discussing making some changes, switching Drew Lee and Tommy Osbourne."

"And from your perspective?"

"I learned a lot, and not just from my klutz show when I tried front tire carrier."

"That was no klutz show. Stepping into something like that for the first time has to be wild."

She smiled at him. "I guess you'll find out next week."

"I guess I will," he agreed. "So what did you learn?"

"That Osbourne is strong, but he forces things instead of working with them. That Calvin Glass made the Olympics in hurdles for a reason, and that Bob Pryor has an amazing way of knowing everything that's going on around him, to the point I think he could do his job blindfolded."

"Almost all good, then," Nathan said.

"Yes."

Nathan turned into the iron gates marking the beginning of the Grossos' property. It was a bit of a drive to the house, itself.

"Llamas!" Stacy cried, pointing at a trio of leggy creatures standing in the fenced field to their right.

"Dean says Patsy fell in love with them several weeks ago, after seeing some at a friend's farm. Now she has her own flock or herd or whatever that might be called."

"They're adorable."

"They spit," Nathan said.

"Well, nothing in life is perfect."

"But some things are darned close," he replied, thinking about how her smiles and her laughter had in just a few days made him feel less trapped and bitter.

Stacy said nothing in return, and he knew that he had come too close to breaching that wall she'd built around herself. Kindness and positive talk she'd give, but she didn't seem to know how to accept in return. All he could do was keep telling her his truths, and eventually she might see that she was worth his kindness, awkward as he was in delivering it.

Nathan pulled up next to the line of cars that had angled up against the white fencing separating the pastureland from the more lushly landscaped property surrounding the Grossos' large but welcoming home.

"Give me one second," Stacy said, reaching down to retrieve her purse. She slipped the elastic from her hair and tucked it into the little bag. With nothing more than a quick combing with her fingers and a shake of her head, her hair fell in a sleek golden swathe to her shoulders.

"Okay," she said.

"Better than okay," Nathan replied, then unclipped his seat belt, opened the door and went around to her side of the car to help her out. He held out his hand to take hers, but she shook her head.

"I'm fine by myself," she said, then scrambled from the car. Her smile shone artificially bright. "Ready!"

She took off for the house, leaving him to close her car door and catch up as quickly as he could. And as he lengthened his stride to reach Stacy Evans, her truth came to him as plain as the edgy tension in her gait: "Get too close and you get left in my dust."

Except this time around, she was facing someone with a will as strong as hers. Nathan would back down for as long as he could, but damned if he'd go away.

CHAPTER SIX

SOMETIMES TOO MUCH was just too much, and Stacy was stuck smack in the middle of such a moment. Nathan excited and unsettled her, the prospect of meeting the Grossos thrilled her, and the idea that her brother might be on the other side of the door in front of which she now stood was plain old freaking her out.

"In a rush?" Nathan asked after he'd joined her on the porch of the beautiful old farmhouse.

"Just keeping up a good pace." She wanted past this crazy moment and out to the other side.

"A good pace for a Chase contender, maybe," he said, then pushed the doorbell.

In a matter of moments the door swung open, and Patsy Grosso welcomed them inside.

"You must be Stacy," she said, holding out her hand. "I'm sorry our paths didn't cross sooner. Life has been hectic."

"I totally understand. It's a pleasure to meet you, Mrs. Grosso," Stacy replied as she shook the older woman's hand. Patsy, who now co-owned the Cargill-Grosso team with her husband, had always been one of Stacy's idols. In a busy and competitive world, she had raised a son who'd become a NASCAR Sprint Cup

Series Champion, made her marriage to yet another such champion flourish, and shown herself a business force with which to be reckoned.

"Please call me Patsy. We're not much for formality around here," she said in a warm voice that eased some of Stacy's tension.

Patsy was casual, but in a lovely, tailored sort of way. She wore dark-colored denim jeans and a pale blue linen blouse that didn't have a crease or wrinkle to it. Stacy had always been awed by women who could wear linen and not look as though they'd just traveled cross-country on a mule, which was what linen did the second it touched Stacy's skin.

"Okay, Patsy, then," she said.

Patsy turned to Nathan. "Nathan, you're looking more relaxed than I've seen you in a good, long time. I wonder what's the cause of that?" Her eyes sparkled as she glanced back at Stacy, who felt color begin to creep up her face.

"Maybe the good business sense to bring Stacy on board at Cargill-Grosso," Nathan replied, with emphasis on the word business.

"Of course," Patsy said. "Welcome to the team, Stacy. I'm sure you'll find that we're quite an intimate group."

In a return volley to Nathan, Patsy had settled equal emphasis on the word *intimate*. Stacy had to smile.

"Stacy, why don't you let me introduce you around?" Patsy suggested.

"That would be wonderful." She needed the space from Nathan and even better yet, if she ran into Kane while standing next to Patsy Grosso, her brother could hardly treat her poorly.

"Make yourself at home, Nathan," Patsy said. "Kent and Dean are out on the back terrace talking shop. Since you're in a *business* mood, feel free to join them."

"I will," Nathan replied.

"Men," Patsy said in a kind yet mildly exasperated tone after Nathan had hightailed it to the terrace. "Sometimes they fail to see what's right in front of them."

"Really, Nathan's and my relationship is strictly business."

Patsy laughed. "And said so earnestly. Some women fail to see what's right in front of them, too. But I promise I won't tease you any more this evening." She looped her arm through Stacy's. "Now let's go mingle."

"Let's," Stacy said. And if fate wanted to grant her one favor on this crazy day, it would be the sight of Kane Ledger….

NEVER UNDERESTIMATE the perceptiveness of a Grosso—particularly a female one, Nathan thought as he stood next to Dean and Kent, sipping a tall glass of iced tea and considering the alternative that he was transparent and Patsy not perceptive at all. Transparency spelled disaster in business negotiations, so he'd stick with the concept that Patsy was well attuned to what he fought to hide even from himself.

Another Grosso joined the group—Kent's wife, Tanya. She settled her hand on Kent's arm and said, "Mind if I steal you away for a few minutes? I have someone I'd like you to meet."

Nathan looked toward the French doors that led back into the house. Stacy was standing on the other side in a smiling and chatting circle of women.

"Steal me away any time," Kent said to his wife, then brushed a kiss against her cheek.

"We're going to go mingle," Kent said to his dad. "Talk to you later, Nathan."

And then the couple headed off, their body language speaking of nothing but newlywed bliss.

Nathan hadn't yet craved the permanency of marriage, but he had to admit that the sort of intimate understanding he saw between Kent and Tanya looked good. The laugh that followed his musing was involuntary; he'd just used Patsy's word...*intimate*.

"Want to share the thought?" Dean asked.

"I was just thinking about how damned perceptive your wife is."

Dean laughed. "It's tough to get much by Patsy. After over thirty years with her, I'm done trying."

Nathan raised his glass in salute. "Smart man."

"Don't you know it," was Dean's wry response.

"Have a few more minutes to talk business?" Nathan asked.

"Probably about thirty seconds," Dean said with a glance toward the house. "Patsy's business radar kicked in when she saw me talking to Kent, and I promised I'd make tonight a business-free zone." He shook his head in a bemused sort of way. "It's funny. I slowed down to make her happy, but I'm finding that it makes me happy, too. I never would have expected it. So, before I'm off to smell the roses again, what is it you wanted to talk about?"

"I was wondering if you or Patsy have looked at any of the résumés for team manager?"

"Résumés?"

Patience, Nathan counseled himself. Short of quitting mid-season and leaving the Grossos high and dry—which he would never do—he had little leverage to push this process any faster.

"You and Patsy both have copies of the résumés on your desks and in your e-mail," Nathan said. "We've got five solid candidates to permanently fill the position. I'd like to have Maria start scheduling interviews." Two weeks ago, they'd had eight candidates, but three had taken other employment while Cargill-Grosso dragged its feet. "We really need to get moving on this."

Dean nodded. "I know, I know…but in a way, it's your fault."

"How's that?"

"You've been doing one helluva job filling the slot temporarily, and once something's on track, it's tough for me to find the need to knock it off. Are you sure you don't want this as a permanent position?"

"Dean, we've been through this. I've been glad that I've been able to help you, and honored that you and Patsy asked, but I have my own company to run and I like doing that."

"Your father would have been tickled to see a Cargill continuing with the team."

Nathan shook his head at Dean's new approach. "That's not exactly playing fair, is it?"

"Sure it is. I'm just using facts."

"Yes, Dad would have been pleased," Nathan said. "But he'd also long ago accepted that I wanted to make my own way in the world. I've put five years of hard work into Liberty Partners. Five more and I'll be on the management consultancy map in a big way." Especially now that he had lost the dead weight of Tom, his cheating partner.

Dean grinned. "You're a competitor, just like your father was. Success tastes good, doesn't it?"

"It does."

"Know what tastes better?"

"What?" Nathan asked.

"Kicking back and enjoying the fruits of all that hard work. I'll get to the résumés once we have both Kent and Roberto showing improvement. And I promise that we'll have a candidate identified ASAP."

"I won't be back next season," Nathan added, giving Dean one last diplomatic nudge.

Dean nodded. "Yeah. Now go enjoy the party, Nathan." He chuckled. "After all, that's what life is about."

Nathan looked to the far side of the large flagstone terrace, where Stacy stood with yet another group of people, laughing and talking. There were, he supposed, worse fates than the company of a beautiful woman at a good party....

KANE LEDGER WAS NOT in the house. Or outside it, either. Stacy was a little disappointed, but in a way, relieved, too. It would have been too much input dealing with his presence on top of all the other people she'd already met. She would just focus on how totally amazing it was to find herself in this place, surrounded by people she'd spent years reading about and watching on television.

Patsy Grosso had been even nicer than Stacy had thought possible. After spending time with her, Stacy couldn't help but wonder how different her life might have been at this point if she'd had a mother like Patsy. And then she wondered if it were really true that Patsy had a daughter other than Kent's younger sister, Sophia. That out there in the world, somewhere, was a young woman who had never gotten to know Patsy's love. She guessed that no matter how beautiful a life might be from the outside looking in, one never knew about those hidden heartbreaks.

"How are you at assembling antipasto trays?" Tanya, Kent's wife, asked, breaking into Stacy's reverie.

"Don't know. I've never tried," Stacy said.

"Well, now's your chance. I had promised Nana, Kent's great-grandma, that I'd help, and I can promise you that no trip to the farm is complete without seeing Nana in action. She's a dynamo, that woman."

As was Tanya, who Stacy knew was one the most in-demand wedding photographers in the Carolinas, and still had no airs about her. Stacy had liked Tanya on sight. Like Stacy, she'd never be mistaken for a tall woman, but there was something about her that was so inviting that she'd never be overlooked. Heaven knows that Kent doted on her.

"To the kitchen, then!" Stacy proclaimed.

As they turned to go inside, she saw Nathan heading their way.

Tanya must have followed her line of vision because she asked, "Not too hard on the eyes, is he?"

"A little tough on the nerves, though," Stacy said, then wished she hadn't. That was a personal comment, and as much as she had loved everybody she'd met thus far, this was business.

"Then he has your attention, I'd say."

"He'd better. He's my boss," Stacy replied just as Nathan intercepted them.

"You've been making the rounds for a while. May I get you something to drink? Iced tea...sparkling water?" he asked her.

"Thank you, but no. Tanya and I are on the way to the kitchen to pitch in on a few last-second details. Maybe you'd like to come along?" she asked jokingly.

From the look of panic on his face, she might as well have asked if he wanted to go down to the stables and muck out some stalls.

"I'll give that one a thank you, but no, in return," he said. "But come sit by me at dinner. I'd like you to meet some of Kent's marketing team."

For the life of her, Stacy couldn't imagine why he'd want her to mingle with marketing, but she agreed anyway.

The trio walked inside together. Then Nathan veered off, away from the route to the kitchen. Tanya's brown eyes lit with laughter. "That's one attentive boss."

"He's just trying to make me feel welcome," Stacy said blandly.

"Sure thing," Tanya replied.

Thankfully, they entered the kitchen before Tanya could get in any more questions or comments.

Villa Grosso's kitchen was beautifully appointed in a way that made its modern conveniences blend with the rustic, homey feel of the house. And just the mingled scents of garlic and pungent tomato sauce from the cooking now taking place were enough to put a pound on a woman's hips.

"Who have you brought me, Tanya?" asked an

elderly but energetic woman who Stacy knew had to be Juliana Grosso. Juliana had raised her grandsons-by-marriage, Dean and his brother, Larry, after their parents had died in a flash flood while camping. The unity and determination of the Grosso family were the stuff of NASCAR legend.

"This is Stacy Evans, Nana. She's working as a fitness trainer for Kent's over-the-wall pit crew."

"Do you like pasta marinara? Antipasti? Homemade bread? Insalata caprese?" Nana asked Stacy.

"Yes to all of the above," Stacy replied with a smile.

"Then welcome to the kitchen. Wash up and lend a hand," Nana said.

"I'd love to."

"Tanya, everything you and Stacy need is set out on the island. Make those platters pretty," Nana directed.

As Stacy and Tanya made arrays of beautiful cheeses and cold cuts around crockery bowls filled with hot and spicy pickled cauliflower and peppers, Patsy flitted in and out, checking on the progress in the kitchen and pitching in to help as much as Nana would permit. This was clearly Nana's show.

"We'll be serving family style on the terrace," Nana said. "Girls, take the antipasto platters out and place them so they're evenly spaced. And get Sophia in here! Being a newlywed doesn't excuse her from helping."

"Yes, Nana," Tanya said, picking up a platter. Stacy followed after with another. They went back outside, weaving through the group, which Stacy counted to be around twenty.

"Sophia," Tanya called to her sister-in-law, "Nana wants you in the kitchen."

Sophia, who was standing with her husband, NASCAR driver Justin Murphy, gave him a kiss on the cheek. "Duty calls. I'll be back."

Stacy followed Tanya to the edge of the terrace, which was surrounded by raised planter beds of the same stone as that beneath their feet. Though Stacy hadn't noticed it earlier, there was a break in the greenery, which marked three broad steps down to another level of terrace. There sat an outdoor dining room that reminded Stacy of her cyber-travels to the vineyards of Tuscany. A beautifully set long wooden table sat in the center of this terrace. Around it were armchairs of the same lovely golden wood. Stacy felt as though she'd fallen into an amazing dream.

"Put your tray at this end, and I'll put mine at the far end," Tanya said. "Then we'll go back and get the other two to take care of the middle." Stacy did as directed, and then made her way back to the kitchen. Patsy and Sophia were on their way out with huge bowls of wonderful looking pasta topped with rich, red sauce. Stacy reckoned that she was going to need to add an hour to her workout tomorrow to atone for the sinful amount of food she planned to eat tonight.

"Don't forget to come back for the bread," Nana directed as Stacy and Tanya hefted their second set of antipasto trays.

"We won't, Nana," Tanya dutifully replied. "It's a zoo here, and I love it," she said to Stacy in a quieter tone.

"I heard that, young lady," Nana lovingly chided.

Family. Stacy hungered for it, and she vowed one day

to have it. But for now she would feed the one appetite she could satisfy and say that for this one day, that was enough.

DINNER WAS winding down, and Nathan couldn't recall the last time he'd felt this relaxed. Certainly it had been before his father's death. It wasn't just that no one at this table looked at him with suspicion. A lot had to do with the woman next to him, the one who'd made friends with everyone she'd met tonight. Nathan was adept in business and smooth in social situations, but sometimes his innate reserve got in the way. Not so with Stacy, and he respected her for her open, happy attitude.

He looked to his right, just to enjoy the sight of her, and caught her watching him.

"I'd say 'a penny for your thoughts,' except you're such a sharp businessman, you'd probably negotiate me up from there," she said in a voice that was meant to carry only to him.

"I'll give you my thoughts for free. I was thinking that you do very well in social situations."

Her eyes grew marginally wider. "Is there any reason I shouldn't?"

Again, they had that disconnect, and he'd insulted her. "No, of course not. None at all."

"Well, then maybe you can take into account my social ease if I come up a little short on the ten percent time reduction."

He smiled at her quick turn of the conversation to her advantage. The more time he spent with Stacy, the more he wanted to know her. "I'll take it under advisement."

Just then, Dean Grosso rose from his place at the

center of the table, opposite Nathan and Stacy, and down a way. He raised the wineglass he held in his right hand.

"First, I want to thank all of you for joining us tonight. It's the best of both possible worlds when co-workers become family, and family becomes co-workers. Thank you all so much for bearing up under the challenge and excitement of our first season at Cargill-Grosso." He looked to his right, where Kent was seated. "To my son, Kent, may you make this the third Grosso championship season in a row." He looked to his left. "And to my beautiful wife, Patsy, may I be so lucky as to have you put up with me for another thirty-plus years."

Laughing, everyone raised their glasses and offered up their good wishes. When people began to push back from the table, Nana rose. "Grosso boys, don't wander off. Cleanup duty is yours. And that includes *you,* Milo," she said to her husband.

Stacy's laugh was richer than even the cannoli they'd just finished eating.

"I love that woman," she said. "I think she could run a small nation with her hands tied behind her back."

"I think you're right," Nathan agreed, then rose and helped Stacy out of her chair.

"Thank you," she said. He liked that response far better than he had her earlier sprint from his car.

She reached down and retrieved her little bag from where she'd slung it over the back of her chair. "We should probably say our goodbyes. We both have an early morning."

They were in his car and on their way back to the

employee lot at Cargill-Grosso well before Nathan was prepared to call an end to the evening. It was, he now knew, not so much a question of if he wanted to kiss this woman, but when. The word *soon* came to mind.

Nathan pulled in next to Stacy's car. Luckily, the ancient thing was once again the only vehicle in the lot, so he didn't have to navigate the diplomatic minefield of "How did you know this was my car?"

"Well," Stacy said. "Thank you for thinking of including me tonight. I'm sure I'll feel so much more at ease at Darlington because you did."

Then why was that note of forced joviality back in her voice?

"You're welcome," he said. "It was a pleasure for everyone you met, I'm sure."

"Yes…well…" She was looking around in a distracted sort of way. "You know, I could have sworn I set my purse on the console between us."

"I put the top back up, so we know it didn't blow out. It probably slipped behind our seats," he said.

"Oh, right…"

She scooted a little closer to look behind his seat at the same time he was moving in her direction to check behind hers. The *when* of that kiss became immediately obvious to Nathan.

Now.

He settled his left hand on her shoulder. She stilled. He came even closer, and she didn't move away, though even in the very dim light he could see doubt on her face. Nathan brushed his mouth against hers, a fleeting kiss that would give her the chance to retreat.

But she didn't.

He kissed her again, and all he could think about was the softness of her lips, pliable beneath his own. When kissing like this, there could be no misunderstanding, only mutual pleasure. And, damn, this felt like an oasis in his arid life.

She drew a choppy little breath and pulled marginally away. *And that's the end of paradise,* Nathan thought.

Except it wasn't.

She came closer and nipped at his lower lip so gently that at first he thought he might have imagined it, except she did it again. He might be slow, but he could take a hint.

Nathan kissed her for all that he was worth. He kissed her to lose his past and live only in this moment. Her mouth was sweet, far better than the confections that the Grossos had served. Those, he could pass up. This, he never could. He cupped the nape of her neck, letting his fingers play in the silk of her hair. And he kissed her as though he never planned to stop.

Which he didn't. This woman was addictive, and not just because of her beauty.

Stacy, however, finally pulled away and leaned her head against the seat, her breath coming as harshly and quickly as his in the close confines of the car. From that, he could take the scant comfort that she'd been as aroused as he. Not quite as good as a kiss that continued forever, but enough.

"This was a mistake," she said. "A huge mistake."

Or maybe not comfort enough, after all.

"Why?" he asked, surprised that he could get the word past the need still gripping him.

"Oh, for a million reasons, starting with the fact that you're my boss."

"Temporarily."

Her chin hitched up a notch. "I choose to take that as meaning because you'll soon be heading back north."

Again, that disconnect. But at least he'd found one way that they communicated very well, indeed.

"Yes, I was referring to my job, not yours," he said.

"Good thing. And before we misunderstand each other again, I'll leave you to figure out the rest of those million reasons why this was bad." With that, she scrambled from his car and flung herself into her own.

As Nathan waited for her to start her car and leave the lot, he tried to calculate how long it would take him to come up with those million reasons. In this case, the word *forever* came to mind. Because for each of those million reasons why kissing Stacy might be bad, he could come up with a million more for why he planned to make it happen again.

CHAPTER SEVEN

COULD IT BE Friday afternoon already? Stacy didn't see how that was possible, though clearly it was. She hadn't seen Nathan this morning, and that had been fine with her. His kiss had shaken her even more than she'd expected. This was no adolescent crush. She was an adult woman with adult feelings, and he was bringing all of hers to the surface—not just desire, but admiration, happiness, and a deep curiosity to know him better.

If she allowed herself to feel as deeply for him as she knew she could, there was no telling how long it would take for her heart to heal when he left for Boston. He'd been plain about his plans from the very beginning. The last thing she wanted was another name to add to her "those who have left me" list. Thus far, it was populated only by her family members, and she preferred to keep it that way.

Stacy's day had grown quiet when most of her over-the-wall crew had left, either for Darlington, because they had other team duties, or to take care of things elsewhere before heading to the track. She had taken advantage of the downtime by coming up with a spreadsheet and system to track pit stop improvements without having to rely upon Harley for the information. He still hadn't warmed to her and, while she didn't think he was the dishonest sort, she knew he'd make obtaining information as tough as he possibly could.

"So how's life here in the hinterlands?" Maria asked from outside Stacy's cubicle before stepping into view.

"Hey, how are you doing?"

"Overworked but also well paid," Maria said. "Since Perry's assistant didn't quite know how to deal with you about travel arrangements, I've taken care of it." She handed Stacy an envelope. "This has your hotel info. You can park there and use the shuttle van we've rented for the team to get to the track. You have a room for tonight and tomorrow night. Sorry about the short notice."

This was a surprise. "Wow, tonight? But the race isn't until tomorrow evening." She knew that most pit crew, unless they were doing double duty, didn't arrive until the morning of race day. She'd expected to fall under that plan.

"There was talk about wanting to be sure that you have an overall picture of a race."

"That was thoughtful." She'd wager that Harley wasn't behind that. More than likely, it had been her guys.

"Also, since you're not authorized for a corporate credit card, I took the liberty of getting you a cash advance for your per diem," Maria said. "I kind of doubted that anyone has gotten around to explaining our expense report procedure."

"Worse than that, it never even occurred to me to ask how I was supposed to eat or have the gas money to get to Darlington." The South Carolina town was less than a hundred-mile drive from Charlotte, but Stacy lived on a painfully tight budget.

"By the way, are you going?" she asked Maria, thinking that sharing a ride and putting fewer miles on Maude made sense.

"No, Nathan has to survive weekends without me, which I know must be tragic."

Nathan...

Maria's joking smile faded. "Hey, are you okay?"

"Sorry. I'm a little stressed, I think." Actually, just the sound of Nathan's name spoken aloud had brought back an all-too-vivid memory of that hot though totally wrong kiss. She had to get past this mix of guilt and excitement, and quickly.

"Anything you'd like to talk about?" Maria asked as she settled into the sole guest chair in front of Stacy's desk.

"No thanks, it's nothing a few extra yoga classes won't take the edge of off," she said, except she knew it was more than that. "Wait...." She shook her head. "I can't believe I'm going to do this."

"What?"

"Ask you an insane question. Nathan has a girlfriend back in Boston, right?"

Please say yes. Please give me a reason to think he's a rat.

"Well, there's this woman, Jennifer, who he goes out with every now and then. Total snot...thinks she's better than the rest of the world. Or at least that would be my opinion if he asked me," Maria said. "But I wouldn't call her a girlfriend, really. She'll call, and he'll go days without returning the call. In the meantime, I get accused of not passing on messages."

"Nice."

"Believe me, it's tempting to live up to her low opinion of me."

"I'll bet," Stacy agreed. "So no girlfriend. How about bad boss behavior or shady business practices?"

Maria laughed. "Incredible! Are you shopping for a reason not to like him?"

"More or less, but with only the purest of motives."

"I'm not even going to ask why, unless you want to share with me, but I will say good luck with that one. Nathan is one of the most ethical people I've ever met. Now, if you're looking for shady business practices, that would be Tom Patricks, his former partner. As far as I'm concerned, the guy should be in jail. Nathan caught him embezzling money from the client trust accounts, but instead of calling the police, Nathan made good on all the money out of his own pocket and, through his connections made sure that the lying, cheating jerk can't get a job as a management consultant anywhere on planet Earth."

So she was falling for a hero. That would make it all the worse when he left her world.

"Hey, don't look disappointed," Maria said. "Once, he did forget to buy my favorite bagel when he made the office bagel run."

"Okay, now we're talking," Stacy said.

"But, to be totally fair, I have to tell you that he's the one who wanted you in Darlington a day early so you could learn the ropes."

"That would fall under the heading of *not* helpful," Stacy said, feeling even more flustered.

Maria's laughter was interrupted by the music of her

cell phone. She slipped it from her skirt's pocket, then glanced at its display.

Maria rose. "It's the man, himself, calling from Darlington. Gotta go."

Stacy tried not to listen as Nathan and Maria talked, so she didn't catch the words. Maria's bright and friendly tone with her boss carried all the same. Stacy wondered if she'd ever find her way back to that place…if she could ever look at him and not think of how it had felt to have his mouth on hers, his heart beating just beneath her palm, and his warm and masculine scent surrounding her. Somehow, she doubted it. One kiss, and she'd lost so very much.

NATHAN AND HIS CELL PHONE had a love/hate relationship. He loved it when he needed it, and hated it when it needed him. It seemed that since he'd arrived at the track in Darlington this morning, the thing—on which he'd set the ringer to vibrate—had been buzzing like an angry hornet. He pulled it from his pocket and checked the instigator of this latest interruption.

Hank Overstreet.

This call, he would take. He excused himself from the conversation among the Smoothtone Music execs, who were Kent's sponsor, and Kent's agent, Kane Ledger. The only reason Nathan was involved was that he liked to keep a finger on exactly how content a sponsor who paid as much as Smoothtone might be.

Once away from the group, Nathan said hello to Hank and then waited for him to jump right in, as was his habit.

"Her name is Elena Cruz," Hank said.

"The server? You've found her?"

"Not exactly, but now at least I've pegged who we're looking for. I talked to friends of hers back in New York and learned that she's not an illegal, but that she does have an ex-husband who has beaten her nearly to death more than once. The guy has made it clear that sooner or later, he's going to finish the job."

"Nice," Nathan said with no small measure of disgust.

"Yeah. I'm in the mood for a little pro bono work and think I might just find this jerk and get him back behind bars."

Which was why Nathan had immediately liked Overstreet. Hank was a man who believed in fixing injustice, and Nathan's situation smacked of injustice, though not as much as Elena Cruz's.

"If you need some cash to help with that, let me know," Nathan offered. Injustice didn't sit well with him, either.

"Will do," Hank said. "But first I have to find her. It took a lot of talking, but just a few minutes ago, her friends finally said that I might want to check the hotels in Miami's South Beach area. Another of her friends moved down that way last year. Problem is, I need to do this fast. According to her friends, Elena doesn't like to stay in any one place more than six months in order to keep distance from the ex. It's May now, which means she must be thinking of moving again."

"So get on a plane," Nathan said. "Now."

"I knew you were going to say that, which is why I'm calling you from the airport. One more thing, though…. The only open seat is in first class," Overstreet said, amusement coloring his usually deadpan delivery.

"This must be your lucky day," Nathan said.

"And just maybe tomorrow's yours."

Since he'd done all he could to draw luck his way, now Nathan could only hope.

STACY ARRIVED at Darlington a few hours later with employee identification in hand and great hopes in her heart. Attending her first-ever NASCAR race was exciting enough. Doing it with full access to Cargill-Grosso's pit and garage area was just too incredible to believe. She'd never had the opportunity to travel or to indulge in luxuries, and this weekend was all of that rolled into one. To top it off, there was an excellent chance that she would cross paths with her brother. She felt as though no goal was unattainable.

She quickly realized that today was to be more like a working vacation than an actual workday. The over-the-wall crew wasn't yet all here, so her duties were nonexistent. After getting the lay of Cargill-Grosso's areas at the track, she'd just wandered, talking to team members and looking for familiar faces from dinner at the Grossos'. The only familiar face she kept seeing was Nathan's, but she'd done a very good job of skirting him.

By early evening, while her enthusiasm for her surroundings hadn't waned, she had begun to wonder if she'd ever spot Kane. She'd managed to check all the public areas she thought he might be around, and had ever so casually strolled by the garage areas of the other drivers besides Kent, whom she knew Kane represented. And all for nothing.

Now she stood with Osbourne and Calvin beside the

hauler. The truck, with its glossy exterior featuring Smoothtone Music graphics and images of Kent Grosso in front of the No. 414 car, was impressive enough. The inside, she'd found even more so. The hauler operated as Cargill-Grosso's nerve center, with both the car that Kent would drive, plus a backup stowed on the upper level of the hauler. On the main level were enough parts to fully fix a car, and all the tools that the garage and pit crews would need. Just past the tool area was a meeting room and control center of sorts, where team members could watch the race on large flat-panel televisions.

It boggled Stacy's mind how much time, thought and effort had gone into making Kent's team run seamlessly. The more time she spent around this sport, the more she respected those involved in it. She could see why Kane had been drawn to it. And again she wondered if she'd find a way to see him.

"Hey, anybody still in there?" Osbourne asked, giving her a verbal nudge.

"Sorry, just woolgathering, though in this warmth, I'd do better to be water-gathering. Do either of you want some water?"

They declined, so Stacy decided to get a bottle of water from the cooler and then do one last wander before the final practice session for tomorrow's race. Stacy pulled up just short of the garage when she nearly ran into Kent Grosso. He stood with another man, chatting.

"Sorry!" she said automatically to Kent, and got a "no problem, Stacy" in return. It was only as she moved past them that she realized her own brother was the man with whom Kent was conversing.

After her systematic search for him this afternoon, here he was, right beneath her nose. She could almost hear her yoga instructor's calm voice saying, "Don't force what needn't be forced. Let yourself find your path in the world."

Apparently this path-finding was a lesson she needed to consider some more. All she knew was at that moment, her heart nearly tripped over itself, it was beating so quickly. *This* was the moment she'd envisioned. *This* was the moment she'd worked toward. All she needed to do was turn back and say hello.

But Stacy couldn't make herself do it. Justifications spun through her brain as her feet carried her farther away from Kane Ledger. He was conducting business, and it was impolite to interrupt. She hadn't adequately thought through her greeting. And then there was her favorite excuse: she wasn't dressed for the occasion. But, hey, any port in an emotional hurricane.

Stacy walked into the noise and activity of Cargill-Grosso's garage with the bottle of water she'd grabbed back at the hauler. She tried to open it, but her hand shook too much to grip the wet and icy-cold vessel.

"Need a hand with that?" asked one of the mechanics.

His hands looked clean enough, and definitely not as shaky as Stacy's, so she admitted that she did.

"Gotta be careful in the sun," he said to her as he opened the bottle and returned it to her. "It will take the strength right out of you before you even know what's hit you."

Stacy nodded. "You're right. Thank you."

At this moment, sunstroke almost sounded better

than her recent discovery that her inner core of strength had degraded to the consistency of a marshmallow. She needed to find a moment to collect herself, and that wouldn't be happening in this den of activity.

Stacy stepped back into the glare of the sun and intentionally looked away from Kent and Kane. After three deep, cleansing breaths and a moment to focus on her good qualities, she started feeling less a coward.

Kane had been her hero forever. For years, his success, first as a lawyer and then as an agent, had been the basis for hope in Stacy's life. If he could make it, so could she. Maybe she wasn't degreed, and maybe she'd never be rich like Kane, but she knew in her heart that they shared one very important trait: determination. How else could they both have survived life with Brenda? And with that link in common, how could this first face-to-face meeting go any way but well?

She looked over to the two men, still locked in conversation. The first piece of good news was that panic did not ensue at the sight of them. And the second was that she now could envision that initial, perilous hello. Kane might be movie-star handsome in a dark and dangerous sort of way, but he was also approachable. Stacy could tell that he was being direct with Kent. He met the driver's gaze head-on and gave him one hundred percent of his attention. These were hallmarks of someone who would at least listen, weren't they?

It looked as though she was about to find out. Kent and Kane were through talking. The two men shook hands, and Kent headed in her direction.

"So what do you think of all this?" he asked her.

"Wild," she responded. Though Kent would never know it, she wasn't referring to the hubbub around them.

Kent laughed. "Just wait until tomorrow," he said, then headed into the garage.

Stacy focused on her brother, only to see that he was taking off in the opposite direction in long and purposeful strides.

"Darn!" Stacy might have been able to visualize that hello, but chasing him down hadn't been part of the picture. She took off after him, all the same.

"Kane," she called when she grew close enough. "Kane Ledger?"

He stopped and looked back her way. When she was only a few feet away, he said, "May I help you?"

His expression was devoid of all recognition. If, in that instant, Stacy had been capable of letting her logic kick in, she'd have accepted what she already knew. He had no reason to recognize her, because he had never looked for her. But she was running on emotion, and this hurt. She was going to have to introduce herself to her own kin.

"Hi, Kane, it's me, Stacy Evans…your sister?"

She didn't know how to keep the pleading from her eyes. She so needed for him to see that she was coming to him with only good motives. If she put good feelings out there, maybe good feelings would come back her way.

Her wishes for a good encounter weren't enough.

His expression, already stern, became downright hard.

"What do you want?" he asked.

"Want? From you?"

He gestured at their surroundings. "What else would you be doing here?"

"I'm here on business. I've taken a job as strength and conditioning coach for Kent Grosso's over-the-wall pit crew."

The curve of her brother's mouth could only be described as a sneer. "That's rich. Why not just admit you're the girlfriend of someone on the pit crew?"

"Why would I lie when it's so easily disproved?" she asked her brother as she flipped over her identification badge, which had at one point or another turned over the wrong way. "I am a Cargill-Grosso employee…end of story."

Kane still looked disbelieving…and unpleasant. "A strength and conditioning coach. How'd you pull that off?"

"Maybe by years of experience as a personal trainer and by interviewing very well?" she suggested.

"Yeah. Right."

"So you think you know better than I how I got my job at Cargill-Grosso?"

"Absolutely. You got the job exactly the same way our mother would snag on to a job for a while…looks and lies. And just like Brenda, you're going to lose this one, once they find out what a manipulator you are."

Stacy nearly staggered under his onslaught. What had she ever done to deserve his hostility? Yes, she looked very much like their mother once had before hard living had dissipated her appearance, but Stacy's resemblance was hardly her fault. She decided that she could continue speaking to Kane only because he still must hurt very much from his childhood to be behaving this way toward her. She could forgive him, but she would also correct him.

"You know nothing at all about me. And honestly, Kane, much as I'd like to get to know you and see if we could have some sort of sibling relationship, I won't be treated this way. Not by strangers and most certainly not by family. Save your rude talk and innuendo for someone else…or better yet, for your own personal contentment, lose it altogether. Bitterness is one nasty poison."

For an instant—one so brief that Stacy nearly missed it—surprise registered on Kane's face. And she was sure that satisfaction was registering on hers. Then the moment was gone.

"You should pitch a talk show," Kane said. "The daytime audiences love that stuff. Me, on the other hand…" He shrugged and walked away.

Stacy didn't care that he'd had the last word. She'd left him with something far more important—the seed of a thought that would now start to grow. She was no echo of her mother, and Kane had best never forget that.

CHAPTER EIGHT

"AND THE GROUNDHOG emerges from her burrow to see her shadow," announced Stephens, the gas man, as he casually leaned against a pillar in the hotel lobby.

Stacy shot him a grumpy look. "Are you saying that I resemble a groundhog?"

"No, but I am saying that we wondered if we were going to have to get the hotel staff to break into your room and see if you had a pulse. Last night, you shut yourself in as soon as we got off the van, and now here you are, just in time to catch our morning ride. I think you might have a little recluse vibe going on."

"I was just catching up on my sleep."

He chuckled. "Twelve hours should do it."

"Let's hope."

Stacy looked around the lobby, but didn't see Nathan. She knew he was staying here because she'd seen his car last night. She'd told herself then that she didn't care if she saw him, but that had been a lie. As tough as she'd tried to be after her encounter with Kane, her spirits had dipped pretty low. If she'd run into Nathan and he'd been nice to her, she'd probably have made a bit of a fool of herself. Instead, she'd retreated to her room, curled up in bed and watched television until she'd fallen asleep. Given her lack of activity, Stephens hadn't been too far off with his groundhog comparison.

"The van's pulling up," Smitty said. "Ready?"

"Sure," Stacy said.

They exited through the hotel's wide glass doors and lined up with the other team members. Stacy was next to get on when Nathan came up beside her. He was more casually dressed than she'd seen him, except when running. Still, it would be a stretch to call his dark blue polo shirt, perfectly pressed khakis and brown yachting shoes casual. She glanced down at her garb of sneakers, blue jeans—her nicest pair, at least—and Cargill-Grosso emblazoned shirt. *This* was casual.

"Good morning. Would you like to drive over with me?" he asked.

While she remained sorely tempted to spend some time with a man who didn't look at her as Satan's offspring, it wasn't sensible to bolster her ego when she knew that their intimacy had to stop. It wasn't especially polite to Nathan, either, and she owed him at least that.

"I'll go with my guys," she said. "I'm sure I'll see you around, though."

He smiled at her, and she couldn't quell the feeling of warmth that it brought.

"Who knows?" he said. "Today you might even speak to me, too."

"Move it along, Coach," Smitty said from behind her.

Thankful for the prompting, she said goodbye to Nathan quickly and got in with the other passengers.

After they reached the track, the day passed in a

haze of activity. Though Harley wasn't crazy about it, Stacy tagged after him for most of the morning, asking every question that came to mind about the process they followed at each race. Eventually he started giving her real answers rather than those of the single syllable variety. She was glad for the notebook she'd borrowed from Perry's assistant. With the excitement swirling around her, she'd never have been able to keep all of his explanations in her head.

That evening, by the time the command came to start engines, Stacy was so wound up that she could hardly hold still. This was the real thing! The over-the-wall crew had suited up in uniforms, gloves and helmets, and was ready for action. She knew from her brief experience how hot it was inside that garb, and couldn't imagine what it felt like to be dressed like that in such a high-intensity situation for three hours and more. She rechecked the stopwatch she wore around her neck, which was the only additional piece of equipment she'd required. Stacy needed to see the guys make at least a marginal improvement.

Right before the cars took to the track for their laps behind the pace car, Tanya, Kent's wife, arrived, along with Dean and Patsy Grosso. Stacy exchanged greetings with them. Tanya and the Grossos opted to head back to the garage area and watch the race from the viewing area atop the hauler, but Stacy wanted to stay up-close and down on the ground. She might lose some of the view, but she'd be in the best position to watch and time the over-the-wall pit crew and to observe Harley and Perry as they conferred on pit strategy. Good reasons, all, plus Nathan was up there, which pretty much sealed the earthbound deal.

The green flag waved, signaling the start of the race. A cheer rose from the enormous crowd, amplifying the excitement that coursed through Stacy. Kent had started in sixth position, and as she watched the early laps, it was clear he was defending his position, and then some.

All the drivers came into pit road on lap thirty. Stacy was so caught up in the action that she nearly forgot to hit her stopwatch as the crew started. Bob Pryor, the jackman, could have taken a tighter path around the car, and Smitty had had a brief hesitation before getting the second can of fuel to Stephens, but beyond that, Stacy thought it looked pretty good. When she checked her watch, though, the stop had actually been two-tenths of a second higher than their average.

"Darn," she muttered as she recorded the time in her log.

The next stop was better, enough so that Stacy was doing a little dance when she recorded the time. Her guys teased her, but she didn't care. When they did better than this three-tenths drop, she swore she'd do a full-out jig for them.

Only moments later something went wrong among the cars following the high groove on Turn Two. Stacy didn't have a clear shot at the action, but she saw enough to know that someone had spun out and that other cars had been involved.

"Kent's in it," she heard one of the team members say.

Her heart began to pound. This was so much more personal than back when she'd just been watching races on television. She knew that most of the time, the worst that happened to the drivers was a few bumps and probably a whole lot of frustration over ending the race that way. Still, it scared her...not that she'd ever admit it aloud.

The cars slowed and bunched up behind Roberto Castillo, the leader, as the yellow caution flag fell. All of the vehicles involved in the tangle-up were able to make it into pit road under their own power, including the No. 414 car. With the amount of body damage, it was clear, though, that Kent was out for the day. Disappointment hung over the pit area like a pall.

"Might as well start tearing down," Harley said to the pit crew. Without much talk among them, they began. Stacy headed back to the garage area. Tanya and the Grossos had come down from the top of the hauler, and Nathan had immediately headed to Castillo's hauler. After confirming that their son was fine, Dean and Patsy left to go watch Roberto, as well, to see if he could hold on to the lead. Though their son was out, Cargill-Grosso still had a contender.

"It has to be tough, watching Kent when there's trouble on the track," Stacy said to Tanya, who, like Stacy, stood on the periphery of the action.

"Today wasn't bad because I could see that he was fine, but it is scary, sometimes," she admitted. "But this is what Kent does. I know he's one of the best, and that helps me a lot. That, and being welcomed into his family."

"Family can be wonderful," Stacy said, though definitely not going from personal experience.

Kent stopped over to see his wife. "Loose stuff," he said to Tanya. "Not the way I wanted this race to end."

Stacy knew that loose stuff referred to the dirt that

naturally tended to accumulate on the outer banks of a track. Sometimes a driver might lose control of the car if he got into it.

Tanya's smile for Kent showed none of the concern Stacy knew she'd earlier felt.

"Good thing there's next week," she said to him.

"A very good thing," he agreed, his eyes alight with the obvious love he had for her. "Come on," he said, holding out his hand to Tanya. "Let's head back to the motor home and a little quiet time."

"You might want to hold that thought," Tanya said. "Here comes Kane. I think I'll head into the hauler and watch some of the race from there. Come get me when you're through talking business, okay?"

"Without a doubt," Kent replied before heading off.

As Kent and Kane began to talk, Stacy refused to look her brother's way.

"Stacy, do you want to come watch with me?" Tanya asked.

She did, just to steer clear of Kane, but that would have been cowardly. She might have her faults, but cowardice wasn't among them.

"Thanks, but I think I'll see if there's anything I can do to help my guys," she replied.

Tanya smiled. "Okay, then I'm sure I'll see you around."

Stacy moved away from Kent and Kane. In the garage, she spotted Osbourne, the front tire changer, who was checking over his impact wrench before stowing it.

Harley had told her earlier today how particular the tire changers were about both the condition and maintenance of their air wrenches. It didn't surprise her considering that their income ultimately hinged on their speed and ability to use the air wrench. In her years watching the sport, many of the muffed pit stops she'd seen occurred because of lug nut issues, either in getting them from the air wrench or smoothly onto the bolt.

"So, everything checks out?" Stacy asked as Osbourne put the tool back into its case.

"Good enough for now. She'll get her regular maintenance on Tuesday," Osbourne replied. "And until then she's all tucked away."

"She?" Stacy asked with a teasing arch of her brows. "Your air wrench is a *she?*"

Osbourne grinned. "Of course she is. Just like my car."

"I don't suppose you've named the air wrench, too?"

"Do you think I'd ever admit it? These guys have enough ammo on me as it is."

Stacy laughed as she imagined the other guys giving tough and muscular Osbourne guff. Stranger things had happened, though. Say, perhaps finding herself feet away from her brother with each of them unwilling to acknowledge the other.

"Wise man. Avoid providing ammo at all costs," she said to Osbourne, who nodded in response.

"No ammo" was a lesson she needed to keep in mind, too. Kane was deep in conversation with Kent. Stacy willed herself not to look his way. But if he approached her, she'd keep her chin high. She'd done nothing wrong yesterday in talking to him. She needed to remember that his behavior was a reflection on him…not her.

"Before we call it a race, I want to talk to you about the exercises you mentioned on Wednesday," Osbourne said. "You know, the ones to improve concentration?"

"Funny you should mention that," Stacy replied. "We'll be starting a new routine when we get home. It's probably different from anything you've ever tried."

"Different can be good. Just having us try out again shook things up. I think a little more shaking up could help."

"I think so, too. Averaged out over the two pit stops, you dropped a sliver of time…about a tenth of a second."

"That's a start," Osbourne said.

"It sure is."

She didn't want to think about how tough it was going to be to achieve the greater drop of more than another second in the three weeks left to her. Still, the deadline loomed like a hulking monster.

"Hey, do you know Kane Ledger?" the tire changer suddenly asked.

Stacy shook off her worries to catch up with the conversation.

"Not really," she replied. Sad, but true.

Osbourne hitched his head in Kane's direction. "I just caught him looking at you like you'd keyed his Porsche or something."

Stacy looked over at Kane, who shot her a brief and angry glare. Stacy's temper began to simmer. How dare he act like this in a public setting?

"He's probably just looking at someone else over here," she suggested in the calmest voice she could muster.

"Okay," Osbourne said, but Stacy could see that he

wasn't really buying it. He looked around as if searching for an excuse to leave. She didn't blame him.

"Think I'll go get a bite to eat," he finally said.

After Osbourne had left, she walked toward her
brother, not exactly sure what she was going to say to
him, except she knew that she had to say something. He
didn't give her the chance.

"Don't even try," he flatly stated when she'd just about
made it to him. That hurt even more than what he did
next, which was to turn his back on her and walk away.

Stacy seldom cried anymore. She figured she'd used
up all of her tears when she was little, before she
decided to grab hold of her life and make it work. But
now she felt an unfamiliar burning in her eyes and tight-
ness in her throat.

Don't even try.

Try? He knew nothing about trying. She had taken
an enormous career risk just for the small chance of
talking to him. She should have stopped seeking crumbs
from his table years ago.

NATHAN WAS CONCERNED. He'd seen Stacy flushed with
passion and spirited with challenge, but he'd never seen
her look as she did now. She wore what he'd call, for
lack of a better description, a smile, but her features
were so rigid that they could have been sculpted from
glass. More startling, she hadn't even noticed him approaching, which meant that she now lacked the time
to hightail it away from him.

He knew he should walk away as he had so many
times over the past two days when tempted to talk to
her. She had set her boundaries, and hard experience

told him that pushing her just made her build those walls all the higher. But right now he'd risk it to be sure she was okay. Whether she liked it or not, he cared about her.

"How did today go for the over-the-wall crew?" he asked as an opening question.

"Pretty well," she said in a tight voice, and then paused to clear her throat before speaking again. "We had a tenth of a second time drop, which doesn't exactly bring us down to the low twelve-second range I need, but I'm still pleased."

"You don't look it. In fact, you don't look good at all," he said bluntly.

"What?"

At last he had her full attention.

"Just calling it like I see it," he replied.

"And here I thought you were a diplomat."

"The better part of diplomacy is knowing when to use it, which would not be now. Do you want to tell me what's wrong?"

She shook her head. "There's nothing wrong."

"You might be able to fool others, but not me. I've seen your real smile, and when I came in here, that, Stacy, was not it."

"Of course it was."

"About as much as a copy of a masterpiece bought at a starving artist's sale is the real thing."

She tilted her head and scrutinized him as carefully as he had her.

"There was a compliment somewhere in there. I think."

Nathan laughed. "Yes, there was. But there was also a question in another form. What's the matter?"

"I told you…nothing."

That last hesitation conveyed far more honesty than her words of denial. "Nice try, but the bluffing won't work with me anymore. I know you too well."

"Do you really think so?"

"I know the taste of you," he said so quietly that no one other than Stacy might hear his words. "I know the soft feel of your skin. I know how your words can sometimes sting, and most of all, I know how hard you fight to hide your vulnerability."

Her blue eyes narrowed.

"Come outside," she said, then walked from the garage without looking back.

Nathan followed even though he knew he wouldn't get far by trying to push into areas she wasn't yet willing to cede.

"Yes?" he asked, once she'd come to stop in a place she apparently deemed safe.

"Our relationship is business and nothing else. That's how it needs to be," she said.

Need and want… They were, in Nathan's mind, two very different concepts. What their relationship *needed* to be had nothing to do with what she *wanted* it to be, or she would have simply told him to get lost. She had just given him more proof of what he already knew. She wanted more.

Nathan was grinning like a fool, and darned if he couldn't school his features back to impassivity.

"*What?* What now?" she asked, clearly annoyed by his happiness.

"That," he said, "is up to you."

CHAPTER NINE

"NO WAY," Stacy muttered to herself as she walked through Cargill-Grosso's parking lot to the magnolia tree that marked her favorite prerun stretching place. She wasn't so crazy about the tree this sun-kissed Tuesday. Sometime between when she'd arrived and when she'd dropped the supplies she needed for the guys' new exercise routine in the gym, Nathan had beaten her to the magnolia.

"Good morning," he said as she approached. "It's a new week. Ready to take it on?"

"Absolutely," she replied. Of course, for the sake of her self-composure, she'd much rather have been doing it alone.

Yesterday she'd puttered around home, unable to focus on any one thing for very long. Even Mrs. Lorenzo, her neighbor, had noticed her level of distraction. Then again, it hadn't been tough to miss when Stacy had taken half of the groceries from the trunk of her car, then left the trunk open and the rest lounging in the midday sun. Good thing Mrs. L had been there to keep her on the straight and narrow. All Stacy had wanted to do was think about Nathan and whether he really did see past the cheery exterior she'd spent years honing.

She glanced over at him, and he smiled. She knew that he wasn't being smug; it was her problem if she perceived his expression that way. Fully warmed up, she started down the driveway, leaving her issues of perception versus reality still unresolved. As Stacy ran, she thought about when she'd realized that a smile was her strongest defense.

She'd grown up among the poorest in an area of Halesboro that was hardly impressive to begin with. Kane had been right about one thing: Brenda never had held a job for long. Either she slept in after a night of binge drinking and was fired, or she just walked away, far more interested in finding someone else to pay her way than to develop any skills for herself. Everyone in town had known who Stacy's mom was, and most everyone had given Stacy pitying looks that made her feel awful. And so she'd learned to smile with such enthusiasm that she'd dared anyone to feel sorry for her.

Stacy stretched out her stride, reveling in the feeling of freedom that running brought. Her past was behind her. Well, except to the extent that she wanted to bring the good stuff like Kane—or at least as she'd imagined Kane to be—into her present. At the sound of footfalls, Stacy glanced back to see that another part of her present—whether she wished it so or not—was catching up to her.

"Relentless," she said under her breath, trying to feel annoyed with Nathan.

Truth was, though, some part of her not only appreciated but was thrilled by his refusal to be pushed aside. She was supposed to be the athlete, and he, the executive, but someone had forgotten to remind him of that this morning. Just because she could, Stacy pushed herself harder.

Now, let's see if he can catch me…

Before she knew it, she was at the point where she usually turned back to the office. Not this morning, though. She'd test Nathan's mettle, and her own.

She knew that her mettle was pretty darned tough, after life with Brenda. Even as an adult who should have known better, Stacy had been sucked in, and more than once. Brenda had always promised that she'd stop drinking and find work in exchange for a place to stay. And each time, Brenda had done so well at first that Stacy had let her hopes rise. Maybe they had finally found a way to have a positive relationship. And then sobriety had become too much for Brenda. The last time Stacy had asked her to leave was also the last time she'd heard a word from or about her mother. Some days she didn't know whether she was more concerned that her mother was in jail somewhere, or that she'd show up at her door and start the whole cycle again.

"How's it going?"

Stacy looked to her left. Nathan had caught her. She got the feeling that he also planned to stay with her.

"How long are you going to keep this up?" she asked.

"For however long it takes," he said. "And when you let me in, Stacy, we both win."

It could be that she had met her match….

NATHAN WANTED a nap. Actually, a nap on a sailboat somewhere in the Caribbean. Last night he'd worked well into the night on Liberty Partners matters. And then he'd come to work and decided to keep up with

Stacy, never mind that she was in better shape than he. All by itself, that run should have been enough to wipe him out. But, no. He'd had to do more.

While Stacy had been in his suite showering, the over-the-wall crew had snagged him for his promised pit stop attempt. He'd done better than Stacy, but probably only because he didn't want her to hear that she'd bested him twice in the same morning. And then when Stacy had been in the gym getting some new program set up for the guys, Nathan had proved himself a sucker for punishment by trying tire changing, jack-man, and gas man. So, yeah, he was wiped out.

Just when he was debating between a nap on the sofa or going facedown on his desk, his phone rang.

"Hello?"

"I need you in the gym. Now."

Nathan could only guess that it was Harley, but the man's voice was a half-octave higher than he'd ever heard it.

"Are you okay, Harley?" he asked.

"No. I'm so far from okay that I might never see it again. Get down here before I lose my whole danged over-the-wall crew."

Nathan hung up and gathered what shreds of energy he could. It sounded as though Stacy had stepped square on Harley's toes this time, and Nathan had to admit to more than a little curiosity as to how.

"I'll be in the gym," he said to Maria as he passed by her desk.

"Good luck."

Nathan briefly halted. "You know what's going on?"

"Nope. Just that Harley screamed at Perry's assistant

when he couldn't find Perry, and then he turned on you."

"Great."

Even though he was bone tired, Nathan sped up his pace to the gym, then came to a halt in the doorway.

The lights overhead were switched off, and the vertical blinds over the wall of windows were partially closed. Was this some sort of light experiment that Stacy was running?

The over-the-wall crew was gathered in an uncomfortable cluster while Harley paced back and forth in front of them. Stacy stood next to the crew wearing the smile that wasn't quite a smile. She felt threatened, and Nathan found himself feeling protective. Not that he'd ever tell her. She'd have him shot dead at dawn for the very sentiment.

"What do you think this is?" Harley asked, waving one wild hand at the floor in front of the mirrored wall.

Eight blue foam mats, each about three feet by six feet, sat on the floor in two rows. Facing them was one more mat. Given Nathan's craving for rest, all he could think of saying was *kindergarten nap time*, but he doubted that Harley would appreciate his humor.

"It's yoga!" Harley growled before Nathan could come up with a more politic response. "She's planning on running some girlie, hippie yoga garbage on my men!"

Nathan assessed the men in question. While some appeared more entertained than others, no one looked nearly as ticked off as Harley.

"It's humiliating! It's brainwashing!" the pit crew coach cried.

Stacy laughed, and Nathan was relieved to see the off-smile replaced by something more genuine.

"Brainwashing?" she asked Harley. "And just what am I brainwashing them to do?"

"Probably some sort of New Age mumbo jumbo," he said in a quieter voice. Apparently he'd realized that he'd overstated matters, but he didn't look ready to back down, either.

"Stacy includes yoga in training sessions with my wife," Drew said. "Carrie says that it has taught her to be more focused."

"That's just great for her," Harley replied. "But she's a girl."

Drew chuckled. "Believe me, I have noticed."

Nathan took a quick glance at Stacy. She looked ready to prove just how tough a girl could be. No matter how much he tried to fight it, the truth stood right in front of Nathan: Stacy was a woman to be admired. And adored, if she'd just let someone take that role.

"Let's park the gender argument for a minute, okay, Harley?" he suggested.

"And let's let me get in a word edgewise," Stacy said. "Nathan, what I've seen from watching the over-the-wall crew both in person and on film is that where they most stand to improve is in flexibility and concentration. Yoga will help with both those aspects.

"I've been taking yoga for almost nine years, and training toward my certification in Anusara yoga for the last three. Trust me when I tell you that I'm well qualified to lead the guys through the basic exercises we'll be doing. And, Harley, this is what a little girlie, hippie brainwashing can do for a person...."

She settled herself on the mat closest to the mirrors, closed her eyes and drew in a deep breath. After a quiet pause, she began to move gracefully through a series of positions, each more sinuous and complicated than the next. She was, Nathan decided, one of the most sensual women he'd ever encountered.

He looked at the other men, to find if they were seeing her the way he was. Based on their more reserved expressions, only he was watching her and simultaneously imagining himself kissing her, touching her. Quite a relief, that.

Stacy finished up with her body straight out behind her, and only one palm touching the mat. It looked almost as though she were floating. She stayed that way longer than he'd ever have thought possible, then held another handful of heartbeats past that. Slowly, she lowered herself to the mat, then sat up, swinging her legs in front of her. She looked proud of herself, almost as proud as he felt of her in that moment.

"So, Harley, want to try it with me?" she asked the pit crew coach.

"I'd pay good money to see that," Calvin said.

"Save your money, Glass," Harley replied. "And let's see if your pit time drops or if you find yourself unemployed."

Calvin merely grinned. Harley's bluster was legendary and largely ignored.

"Good luck," Harley said to the men. "She's gonna bend you up like a bag of pretzels, and don't come whining to me after she's done it."

After Harley walked out, Stacy took Nathan aside.

"Thank you," she said.

"For what?"

"For the same thing as last time. You stood up for me."

Nathan loved being a hero as much as the next guy, but he felt that a guy really had to deserve it before taking the accolades. "And just like last time, there's nothing that happened in there that you couldn't have done without me."

"All the same…"

"Okay, you're welcome," he said, knowing that fully embracing her worth was a battle Stacy would win over time, not overnight. If it were a perfect world—which it wasn't—he would know her when she won. Because when that day arrived, she was going to be unstoppable.

ALL IN ALL, the training session had gone very well, Stacy decided as she rolled up the yoga mats and tucked them under a low bench on the gym's mirrored wall. Her guys had quickly grasped the concept that even the simplest of yoga poses took more core muscle control and concentration than they would have expected.

Best of all was the talk they'd had after their cooldown session. After watching Harley's outburst, they had realized that whatever their private reservations about this workout might be, all were founded in lack of knowledge. She loved the fact that these men, for all their macho attitudes, were open to change.

Stacy had just finished putting away the mats when the phone on the gym wall rang. She hesitated for an instant before answering, sending a prayer into the universe that this wasn't grumpy Harley on the other end, or some other bit of frustration to take the shine off her day. Either way, she had to answer.

"Hello, fitness center," she announced, since it sounded so much better than gym.

"Stacy?"

She knew this voice but couldn't place it.

"It's Kane."

"Hello, Kane."

She'd kept her voice neutral, though it had been difficult. She couldn't imagine what else this man might have to say. Short of picking on her for her height, there was nothing he hadn't already insulted about her. She supposed that was good news of sorts.

"Is there something I can do for you?" she asked.

"No, not really.... I just wanted to say that you were right. I don't know you. I had no business judging you."

She'd known he couldn't have believed his behavior appropriate. She'd doubted, though, that he would apologize. Beneath his smooth exterior, he seemed too angry to ever back down. What drove the anger, she could only guess.

"Well, thank you for that," she said.

"It's what I owe you," he said.

Stacy considered what, in some way, she owed him. "I want you to know that I want nothing from you other than a few minutes of your time every now and then," she said. "From the times we've seen each other, I've gotten the feeling that you think I have some other agenda. I suppose when you get to a certain financial position in life, you can't help but think—"

"It's not like that."

He quieted for a moment, and Stacy wasn't sure what to do next. Talking to him was like negotiating a minefield.

"You look like her, you know."

She exhaled a slow breath. "I know I do. But I'm not Brenda."

"I know… I know. I just reacted, that's all. It was wrong of me."

She sat silent. There was no point in rubbing his nose in a mess that he already recognized as a stinker.

"So…you're well?" he asked.

Stacy couldn't help but smile at the stilted conversation. What did one say to a sibling he'd left behind over twenty years ago? *So, what have you been up to?* was a little broad to cover, after all.

"I'm doing great," Stacy said.

"Good…I'm glad."

"Thanks."

An uncomfortable silence crept over them again.

"Hey, I should get going," Kane finally said. "But maybe if you gave me your e-mail address or something…?"

"Sure," she replied, then gave it to him. She didn't bother reminding him that his secretary probably already had it, since she'd tried to contact him by e-mail last year, too.

"Take care of yourself, Kane," she said.

"Yeah, you, too. I'm sure I'll see you around."

After they had said their goodbyes, Stacy held the phone for a moment longer before putting it back in its receiver, just to stretch out the interlude. She knew better than to think Kane would now welcome her into his life, but these crumbs she would take and enjoy.

CHAPTER TEN

ON WEDNESDAY MIDMORNING, as was his habit, Nathan took stock of his week thus far. One thing was certain. He had exercised his patience far more than he had his body.

Since he and Stacy had worked themselves all the way up to a polite standoff, they had toned down their morning runs to something less than a death march. She even laughed and joked with him, but declined every invitation for more time together. He'd be taking it personally, except he could see that it was growing tougher and tougher to turn him down. Patience wasn't his favorite virtue, but he was learning to embrace it.

The willingness to outwait a situation had been key in another area, too. During the activity of the race weekend, it had been easy to put aside thoughts of Hank Overstreet down in Miami. Here, though, in the quiet of his office, Nathan couldn't let go of the issue. No news might be good news in some situations, but not in this one. All the same, he had to know.

Nathan scrolled through the contacts on his cell phone until he came to Hank's number, and then placed the call. Overstreet answered on the fourth ring. Wherever he was, country music blared in the background.

"I'm guessing you're not still in Miami," Nathan said.

"Oklahoma City," the investigator replied. "And don't worry, it's not on your dime. It's for another client."

Nathan knew that obviously he wasn't Hank's only client. He wished he were, though, if that sort of attention could bring his time dangling at the end of a noose to a positive end.

"So, no luck in Miami, I take it?" Nathan asked.

"I'd call it more of a no-resolution situation," Overstreet replied.

"No resolution, *yet,* don't you mean?"

"Look, I still feel that we're going to find Elena Cruz, but it's going to take time. And how much time, I can't tell you. Someone who doesn't want to be found is a pretty tough target. I've checked all the hotels around Miami, and let me tell you, they have their share. No luck, though."

Nathan absently rubbed at his forehead, trying to quell the headache that had begun.

"What's the game plan from here?" he asked Hank.

"I follow up a few more Miami leads, then talk to the New York friends yet again. They know more than what they've said. They're protecting her, and I can't say I can blame them."

Nathan couldn't, either. All the same, though, he needed Elena Cruz to speak the truth so he could get this part of his father's death behind him.

"I understand," Nathan said. "But do me a favor and at least e-mail me a no-news update, if that's the case."

"Will do," Overstreet replied. "And in the meantime, keep moving on, Nathan. We both know you didn't have anything to do with your father's death, and the more time you spend dwelling on this, the worse you're making it on yourself. Get out there and live, okay?"

That, Nathan could and would do.

STACY DIDN'T WANT to overreach and call the past few days miraculous, but they sure as heck had felt that way. The latest practice pit stop times she had on the guys were amazing. The over-the-wall crew had dropped over a second! Add to that the couple of casual e-mail exchanges she'd had with her brother about recent NASCAR events, and she felt charmed at the very least.

"That must be some incredible yogurt, the way you're grinning at it," Calvin said as he pulled up a chair by Stacy's in the lunchroom, where she was having her morning snack.

"The yogurt is good. You guys, on the other hand, have been incredible in practice!"

Calvin smiled. "Could be that your enthusiasm is catching on."

"Or it could be the yoga," Stacy said.

He shook his head. "Give yourself some credit, Coach. You're one heck of a motivator."

She could feel a blush rising on her skin.

"Thank you," she said, ducking her head a little, though she knew there was no hiding her response.

"Didn't mean to embarrass you," Calvin said, his voice a little gruff. Now she'd embarrassed him!

"Well," he said, after taking a long swallow of his energy drink. "If we keep this up, we keep you around, right?"

"That's right."

She'd have to find referrals for her last few private clients, but Stacy was ready for the change...not to mention a job with benefits and a measure of security. Since Calvin was a full-timer, she decided to take the optimistic approach and ask him a few questions about company benefits. He mentioned the health insurance plan and vacation and sick pay, all of which sounded like paradise to Stacy.

"Oh, and one more thing. I just heard that the Grossos have decided to keep on with the tuition reimbursement plan that Alan Cargill had in place," Calvin added.

"Tuition reimbursement?"

He nodded. "Yeah. Cargill-Grosso will reimburse tuition and book expenses for any classes we take toward a job-related degree. I've been thinking about going back for my master's degree once I'm not spry enough to work over the wall."

"Well, let's hope that won't be for a while." Calvin was only in his late twenties.

He laughed. "I think I can hang on for a while longer. How about you? Do you ever think about going back to school?"

"I had looked into it," Stacy admitted. "I just could never quite figure out how to afford college without going into a whole lot more debt. I just bought my own place a few years ago, which was tough enough, since I'm self-employed."

"Not for much longer," Calvin said, then pushed back his chair. "If you want more school, look into it, Coach. Might as well take full advantage of what's being offered to you."

That thought stayed with Stacy while she sat at her

desk going over the team members' individual time report. College had always been something for other people, not for her. Before she'd graduated from high school, she'd dreamed of having the name of the college she'd be attending in the graduation program. She'd also dreamed of having her brother at the ceremony. Neither had been possible. But all these years later, her possibilities were growing.

Just past noon, Stacy could take it no more. She logged on to the Internet from the computer at her desk…or at least tried to. After crawling beneath the desk to look for loose cables, she decided to cut her losses and find someplace else to do a little research. Maria seemed to be a logical first stop, but she was having a working lunch, trying to catch up on some Boston business matters for Nathan. She was about to turn and go when Nathan exited his office.

"I'll be back around two," he said to Maria without looking up. When he did, and saw Stacy, his smile made her heart beat faster.

"Hey," he said to her. "Having a good day?"

"Very good," she said. Seeing him always made it a little better.

"Nathan, as long as you're going to be out, do you mind if Stacy uses your computer for some quick research? Hers is acting up," Maria said.

"No, really, that's okay," Stacy quickly cut in. "I can find someplace else to do it." She never would have asked this of Nathan on her own. It was too intrusive.

"It's no problem," Nathan said. "Go on in and make yourself at home." He glanced at his watch. "I have to run…lunch with Dean and the Smoothtone Music guys." And with that, he was gone.

"I can't believe you asked him that," Stacy said, once she was sure Nathan was out of earshot.

"Why? He's just a guy, and it's just a computer. Besides, I think he kind of likes you," Maria added with a cheeky grin.

Knowing there was no graceful way out of that line of discussion other than to retreat, Stacy murmured some vague thing to Maria, then headed into Nathan's office. She settled behind his desk and nudged the mouse to awaken his computer. After typing a few relevant words into a search engine, she clicked the submit button. An array of results popped up even before she had a chance to draw a breath and prepare herself for this new step she was taking.

Stacy's hand shook a little as she moved the mouse to select the first possibility. As the Web site page loaded, she asked herself why she was feeling queasy, and had no good answer.

Easy. This would all be so easy.

The University of North Carolina at Charlotte—right in town—offered a Kinesiology and Exercise Physiology program. All she would need to do was apply for financial aid and then pay it back when reimbursed by Cargill-Grosso.

But if it would be so easy, why was she feeling so ill?

All Stacy could think of was Brenda, who never once encouraged her to study. Actually, she'd done just the opposite. Stacy must have been in eighth grade when her mother had made it clear what she considered Stacy's career path to be.

"With looks like you're gonna have, sweetie, why bother so much with the books?" Brenda had asked. Stacy had still studied, but maybe not as hard as she might otherwise have done, because in what had probably been a passing comment from her mother, Stacy had heard something else…something that had settled in her sensitive mind and taken root. She'd heard that along with not being as rich as most of the kids, and along with having not such a great home, maybe she wasn't all that smart, either.

In time, she'd gotten past it. She was a pro at getting past things, after all. She had graduated from high school with a fairly solid 3.1 grade point—not quite Harvard material, but good enough.

Or had it been all that good, really? What was it going to do for her now?

She'd been out of school for ten years. She'd never even taken the ACT or SAT and had no idea how to study for one, now. Why was she even thinking about trying to go to college? She'd be older than everyone else and totally out of her element. Why set herself up for failure like this?

Sick at heart, Stacy exited out of the search and left Nathan's office, where she should have never, ever been.

THAT NIGHT, Nathan shook his head at the sight of Stacy's car in the parking lot. He might work late, but she worked later. On impulse, he turned heel and headed for the gym. He craved time with her as he never had from any woman. He didn't think it was just her neat trick of holding him at arm's length that kept luring him in, either. This attraction—this need to know her—ran deeper than any game.

As he'd suspected, the gym lights were on. He hadn't quite expected the ticked-off-woman-style country music blaring from the radio, but okay. Stacy was on a treadmill, running at a full-out pace. He called hello so as not to startle her. She glanced his way but kept on running. Her face was tight with concentration and something else he couldn't identify but didn't like. He walked over to the radio and turned it down.

"So, just getting in a last few miles?" he asked, keeping his voice light.

"Exorcising a ghost," she said.

"Interesting approach."

"It works…when I'm not interrupted."

"Keep up that tone and I'm going to think that I'm bothering you," he joked.

"You are. Want to turn the music back up?"

This wasn't the sunny Stacy he knew.

"Maybe in a minute," he replied.

And on she ran.

"So, do you want to talk about this ghost?" he asked once a few more minutes had ticked by.

"Where did you go to college?" she asked instead.

"Princeton."

"Graduate school?"

"Harvard, with high honors."

"And I suppose you went to one of those snooty prep schools, too?"

"Yes." He tapped into the patience he'd been pretty sure he'd used up earlier today. "Stacy, what is this about?"

"Just getting your pedigree straight," she said. "Want to hear mine?"

Given her present mood, he wasn't so sure it was wise to push this any further, but he truly, genuinely, did want to know about her, so he set caution aside.

"Sure," he said. "Tell me something that's not on your résumé."

"Father…split before I knew him. Mother…alcoholic and highly manipulative. Brother…pretty much estranged," she said, and pushed herself to an even faster pace on the treadmill.

He took the information in, and looked at the woman in front of him. He saw the anger and he saw the pain, but he knew he saw something she seemed to be overlooking—her amazing, beautiful determination.

"You've told me something about your relatives, but nothing about you," he pointed out.

Her eyes narrowed. "We're the product of our environment, aren't we?"

"Not necessarily," he replied. Now didn't seem the best time for a "nature or nurture" debate.

"I am, and don't you ever doubt it," she said flatly.

"Gotcha." He was nearly tempted to turn up the music again, except he could see that she was hurting— really hurting—and he wanted to find some way to make her feel better. "If it makes you feel any differently about me, it wasn't all rosy for me, either. I asked my father to send me away for school because I was tired of his obsession with racing. I figured I was better off being absent altogether than having to deal with an emotionally absent dad."

"Poor little rich boy," she said. "Is this the part where I'm supposed to feel sorry for you?"

"Right," Nathan said. Maybe he'd caught her mid-exorcism, and she would come out the other side a little less brutal.

"Maybe you'd do a little better if you focused on your issues instead of me, don't you think?" he asked.

Forget the academic pedigree. Common sense told Nathan it was time to go. And so he turned up the music and left Stacy to her "gonna get even" country song. It seemed that at the moment she had her target dead wrong. He didn't know who it should be, but he was darned well not it.

THE DOOR HAD scarcely closed behind Nathan when guilt kicked Stacy square in the teeth. She'd just been pretty much the poster child for Women Behaving Poorly. Never before had she tried so hard to provoke a fight. And to have done it with someone as nice as Nathan was inexcusable.

Without another thought, she turned off the treadmill and ran out the door. She soon spotted Nathan on the edge of the employee parking lot.

"Hey," she called.

He looked back and stopped, so she slowed from a sprint to a jog.

"I'm sorry," she said, once she was in front of him, close enough that even in the dim light she could read the frustration on his face. "I was being horrible. I don't know what came over me."

"It's okay," he said.

She wrapped her arms around herself, not sure whether the impulse came from the chill settling into the night air, or because she felt so totally miserable.

"No, it's not okay," she said. "Not at all. You deserve far better than that from me."

"We all have our moments. I'd be kidding you if I told you that I didn't," Nathan replied.

"I know, but even at my worst, I'm usually not that bad."

"Do you want to talk about it?" he asked, his voice so kind that her heart ached a little more.

"I don't think that would be a good idea. Besides, it's stuff I should be able to handle by myself."

"And eventually you will," he agreed. "But sometimes the best first step is to talk to someone else."

"Sometimes, but not this time," she said as firmly as she could, considering that she wanted to be in his arms at this very moment. She wanted him to tell her that in the end, everything would work out.

"Why not?" he asked.

"It's personal and kind of messy…definitely embarrassing."

He shook his head. "So? *We're* personal."

And they were, whether she kept fighting it or not. She had begun to fall a little bit in love with Nathan Cargill from the moment she'd met him, and a whole lot more since then. But this love, like her self-doubts, she planned to keep to herself.

She was about to say something to him—some lame sort of good-night—when he reached out and pulled her into his arms.

"Don't argue the point," he said, and then kissed her so long and deeply that Stacy thought if she opened her eyes, she'd see the stars circling in the night sky.

Stacy wanted to take this moment into her soul…to have something to hold on to when self-doubt crept back in. This amazing man cared for her, desired her, even put up with her bone-deep stubbornness. If he didn't doubt her, why did she keep on doubting herself?

When he paused for a moment, she drew him back to her, giving him with her body what she could not give in words. He made a sound of hunger deep in his throat. If only she were taller, she would have fitted her body to his and let him feel how much she hungered, too.

The interlude ended long before she was ready. When they heard someone off in the distance clear his throat, they drew slightly away from each other. Too dazed to stand on her own and slightly embarrassed, Stacy hid her face against Nathan's chest.

"Night guard," Nathan murmured into her ear. "It's okay."

He held her for a moment longer and, when he let her go, Stacy got the feeling that it hadn't been easy for him to do.

"It's probably a good thing he came along when he did," Nathan said. "It's not the best place for me to have started this, is it?"

"Probably not," Stacy admitted. Not that she had cared while he had been kissing her. All she had wanted was more.

"Do you think you can agree now that what we have between us is personal?" he asked.

She nodded. To deny it would have been crazy.

"Then do you think maybe we can get beyond all the worries and reasons that on paper this makes no sense, and just enjoy our time together?"

"I'll try," she said. But Stacy knew herself well. This would be her greatest challenge yet.

CHAPTER ELEVEN

STACY'S THURSDAY had begun undeniably well. Nathan had joined her for their prework run. But unlike any prior morning, when they'd come to their customary turnaround point, he had taken her into his arms and kissed her until they were breathless.

"Just keeping it personal," he'd said when he was done, then kept pace with her all the way back to headquarters. And unlike before, he'd stayed in his suite while she'd been in the shower. Now, as she finished applying her mascara and lip gloss and checked her reflection in the bathroom mirror, Stacy had to admit that she loved the thought of finding him out there when she was done.

When she stepped back into his office, he looked up from his computer and smiled. "You look beautiful."

She was trying to learn to take his compliments in stride. No longer would she search for an untruth or an ulterior motive.

"You're pretty darned sharp, yourself," she said. Of course, he was still in his running clothes, awaiting his turn in the shower, but she liked him a little scruffy around the edges. He seemed more accessible when he wasn't wearing his corporate best.

"Thank you," he said. "But I should probably change before I take you out to dinner tonight, don't you think?"

"Dinner?" she echoed.

He shook his head in mock dismay. "Is that communication problem coming back? Dinner…you know? The meal after lunch?"

Stacy smiled at his teasing tone. "I recognize the word."

"Good. How about right after work? No place fancy, just a chance to be somewhere away from this crowd. We don't seem to get much—or any—of that."

"I like that idea…very much."

"And I like you…very much," he said.

The warmth in his eyes had taken on a new depth. She'd never had a man look at her this way, and it sent a delicious and slightly scary thrill through her. This was all so new and so fragile that she didn't want to see it shatter.

"Thank you," she said, since an *I love you* in return, while honest, remained impossible.

He smiled. "'Thank you?' I'll take that as a response…for now."

"Thank you," she said again, automatically, then burst into laughter when she realized what she'd done. "I promise that before dinner, I'll work on something new to say."

"Even if that's all you say, I'm looking forward to it."

Before she summoned up yet another awkward thank-you, Stacy said goodbye. After a few minutes of morning chat with Maria, she left the office building.

As she came out from under the shade of the portico, she saw Kane heading her way.

Stacy steeled herself. These face-to-face meetings remained awkward. She was coming to much prefer the e-mail approach with him. Though she was sure he didn't mean to, Kane intimidated her. She wondered if everyone could sense the anger he carried, or if being a sibling somehow made her more conscious of what rested beneath that handsome, hotshot exterior.

"Good morning," she said, prepared to move on.

"Good morning," he answered, then stopped when he'd come even with her. "Are your guys ready for this weekend?"

Saturday's race was in Charlotte. The over-the-wall pit crew was especially stoked because the format for this one was different, and even included a special challenge for the pit crews tonight. Competitors that they were, although this was their first year as a team, her guys had been talking big all week about winning it.

"They're looking great," Stacy said, "but you never know for sure until they're in the thick of action. There are so many variables. I remember last year, watching Justin Murphy's gas man almost not get the can out in time. You know he'd practiced that move countless times, but in that one instant, a variable changed."

Kane looked a little bemused. "You really are a fan, aren't you?"

"Since childhood," she said, not adding that she'd become an even bigger fan when Kane's name had started popping up. "How about you? Did you watch when you were little?"

His expression hardened, and Stacy realized that her brother was as skilled at building walls as she.

"I don't know that I was ever little," he said. "Brenda didn't leave me much time for that."

She searched for a positive spin on the truth that she, too, had shared. "Which meant that you thrived as soon as you were on your own, right?"

Kane's laugh didn't quite ring true. "More like survived, for a while there. And I think you inherited the family's full dose of sunshine."

"Could be," she said. "I never saw the point in wallowing in my circumstances."

"That we have in common," Kane said.

Stacy debated whether to ask a question that had been burning inside her since they had first talked. Since he'd brought up the general topic, she decided to go for it.

"Do you ever hear from Brenda?" she asked.

"Once," he said flatly. "About a year ago. I didn't take the call."

That had been around the time she'd last asked Brenda to leave. Her mother must have been desperate for a place to land. Guilt nipped at Stacy, even though she knew she'd done the right thing. She'd talked to a therapist, understood all of the issues, and refused to be an enabler. Even so, that didn't mean that she had to flat-out reject all that her mother had been.

"She wasn't totally bad, you know," Stacy said. "She really felt things deeply and tried to love us."

"You, maybe," Kane replied. "But not me. Never."

"That can't be true. You were her son."

"That relationship is one corpse I have no interest in dissecting, okay?"

A chill crept through her at the harshness of the image and the anger in his voice. She'd mentioned bitterness to him once, but with little effect. She knew better than to try again, especially when he was clearly spoiling for an argument with her.

Stacy pinned on a smile, then made a show of checking her watch. "Hey," she said. "I need to get going. Lots to do before over-the-wall practice, you know?"

As she walked away, she could feel those tears starting again. Having no family had hurt, but trying to regain one was proving to be misery, too.

As FAR AS "real" first dates went, Nathan planned to ignore Thursday night's with Stacy and take a do-over. He'd picked the perfect place, so he couldn't fault the location. Stacy had been charming; no mid-exorcism behavior had been displayed. The evening had tanked because of him, and only him. He'd gotten himself so wrapped up in something he didn't know how to say, that he'd said close to nothing at all.

Nathan had needed to find a non-stalkerlike way to say, *Hey, I looked out my window and saw you with Kane Ledger this morning. Whatever was going down didn't look like small talk between strangers to me. Want to share?*

Or he'd needed to butt out.

However, he hadn't been able to do either.

Instead, he'd sat there and spun out scenarios for what might have been such a tense topic between Kane and Stacy. Eventually, and after much lack of chat on his part, he'd made a vague reference to having seen Kane at headquarters, with the hope that Stacy would just spill. She didn't, of course. Instead, she'd nodded and taken another sip of her wine. And since the whole Stacy/Kane situation was really none of his business, he'd let the topic rest. But he hadn't stopped obsessing. Were they former lovers? Was she still seeing him?

Now, two days later, he was almost ready to let it go. And that was only because work had absorbed him to the point that he'd had to shelve his curiosity. He'd never been in this situation before—so attracted to a woman that he could hardly push her from his thoughts. Though there was no rational reason for it, this morning he'd gone miles out of his way to pick her up at her home and bring her to the track. All because he craved time with her…and wanted to be sure she felt the same about him. And *only* him.

"Impressive self-control, Cargill," he muttered to himself as he walked back toward the hauler and Kent's pit stall. The all-star race was due to start in a couple of hours, and even he had to enjoy the excitement thrumming in the air.

As Nathan neared the hauler, his pace slowed. There was an unwelcome face among those he knew. It had been months since he'd seen Lucas Haines, the NYPD detective assigned to his father's case. Nathan could have used a few months more.

Haines was deep in conversation with Dean and Patsy Grosso. It was sheer paranoia on Nathan's part to think that Haines would be trying to poison the Grossos against him. But after over six months of having been viewed as a criminal, Nathan figured he was entitled to a little paranoia. And it wasn't paranoia to think that Haines was the current center of attention in the pit area. That was cold, hard fact.

Nathan joined the Grossos.

"In case you've forgotten who I am," Haines said, as he pulled out his badge, then flipped it open.

The unnecessary gesture drew yet more attention. Even Stacy, who was normally so focused on her team, now watched. Nathan's gut tensed at the thought of the gossip that would grow from this visit. He reminded himself that he had nothing to hide and nothing to be ashamed of.

"I know who you are, Haines."

"Just following protocol," the detective responded. From the glint in the man's eyes, Nathan could tell that he planned to play this one as though he were on a Broadway stage.

Patsy looped her arm though Dean's. "Well, Detective Haines, perhaps you'd like to go into the hauler, where it's quieter and more private? Since you don't need us anymore I believe we'll be on our way."

Dean shot Nathan a concerned glance.

"I don't think Mr. Haines will be here much longer," Nathan assured the couple, while intentionally ignoring Haines's title to annoy him.

"Come see us before the race starts," Dean said.

Nathan nodded his agreement, then focused on Haines.

"So what brings you here?" he asked.

"It's funny, Cargill, that the only time we have contact is when I come looking for you. It seems an innocent man would be hunting me a little more."

"Possibly. Or maybe an innocent man wouldn't feel the need to be in constant contact."

"That would be the wrong choice, though, wouldn't it?"

"Look, Haines, it's not as though my father's murder is ever far from my thoughts. Believe me, even if you hadn't decided to add me to your suspect list, I'd still have a whole lot more reason to want to see this solved than you would. He was my father, and I loved him."

"From a distance, mostly," Haines commented.

Nathan bit back on his frustration and offered up honesty. "My relationship with him wasn't perfect. We had our issues." He gestured at the sea of activity around them. "But I got over it, obviously. I was helping my father with the sale of his business when he died, and I've been helping out Dean and Patsy Grosso since then. That's not the behavior of someone who just killed his father out of some bizarre hatred, is it?"

Haines shrugged. "Not according to you. But don't forget that we both know you've been in a tight financial spot, much as you've tried to keep it private."

"So if you know about Tom Patricks, you also know I've been able to cover the losses from his thefts, and without any money that was my father's."

Haines drew a sharp hissing breath between his teeth. "Wow," he said in mock sympathy. "That had to hurt even at your income level, didn't it, Cargill?"

Nathan knew he was taking the wrong tack with this guy. There was no talking Haines out of seeing him as a suspect. Only an alibi would clear him.

"Yes, it hurt, but I'm pretty sure I still have more assets than, say…*you*. Now ask me your questions, and then leave."

"Good enough," Haines said, apparently unruffled by this entire exchange.

Nathan wished he could say the same.

"So, how goes the hunt for an alibi?" the detective asked.

"The alibi exists. This is a hunt for a person…as you know."

"Really? Want to give me the update on your sad tale?"

"Not really," Nathan said. "But just to humor you, here's the short version of what I've found. You want to talk with my alibi, finish tracking down a woman named Elena Cruz. That's the real name of the waitress I was talking to when my father was killed." He reached into his back pocket, pulled out his wallet and handed Haines a card. "This is the private detective I've been using. Give him a call if you have any questions."

Haines flipped the card back at him. "It's not my job to track down your alibi, Cargill. That's your issue. And of course, then there's my take on this whole scenario…."

"Which would be?"

"You've had months to make your alibi all glossy and credible, and you've almost got it down pat. Slow but steady wins the race, eh?"

Nathan had never been a brawler but he was just about ready to give it a try. "Slow doesn't win any race, Haines. Honest, hard work does. I've been honest with you and gotten a face full of attitude back, so unless you're here to arrest me, leave."

"You know why I don't like you, Cargill?" Haines asked.

"No, why?"

"Sounds weird, but it's because we're two of a kind. We're both always right, except in this case, one of us

has to be wrong. Nothing personal, but I think it's you."
He gave Nathan a mocking smile. "See you around."

Nathan hoped not.

TWO HOURS UNTIL race time, and all was well…with
Stacy, at least. She had tried not to eavesdrop as Nathan
had argued with the man with the badge, who one of
the mechanics later told her was the police detective in
charge of Nathan's father's case. The mechanic and
plenty of others on the team had been ready to tell her
a whole lot more, except Stacy hadn't wanted to hear.
Not from anyone but Nathan, and then only if he chose
to tell her.

Stacy wiped the back of her hand across her forehead. Not only was it warm for a mid-May evening, but
she'd been feeling a little claustrophobic. As much as
she loved racing and all the action, right now the pit area
felt like an overcrowded goldfish bowl. Hazel, her fish,
had it far, far better than this. Stacy decided to head into
the hauler for a little quiet time. But when she turned,
she found herself nearly toe-to-toe with Kane. Yes, this
was one crowded bowl.

"Sorry," she said to her brother.

He looked past her, which, admittedly, wasn't tough
to do, considering he was nearly a foot taller than she.

"Hey, Kane," she said, trying again. She knew she'd
been a little abrupt in her leaving when she'd last seen
him, but that shouldn't make a girl invisible.

He went to walk past her, but she danced back into
his way. "Look, if you don't want to say anything more
than hello, I'm fine with that, but I don't like you pre-
tending that I don't exist."

"Okay. Hello," he said, then skirted her again.

Now he'd really ticked her off. Stacy followed hot on his heels. "Nice try, but unlike Brenda, I'm not going to disappear just to make your life easier."

Kane wheeled around, and Stacy nearly smacked into him, she'd been following so close.

"Whatever it is you want to say, say it. I've got people to talk to and business to conduct," he snapped.

She looked around to see if anyone was paying attention to them. Nathan was standing by Dean and Patsy, closer to the hauler. Kent and Perry were by the pit wall, deep in discussion. The team all seemed to be occupied, too.

"Is it so tough to have me like you?" she asked her brother in a quiet voice.

"Yes."

She'd asked the question rhetorically, and his answer threw her for a loop.

"Hey, it shouldn't come as any shock. After all, you were my childhood hero," she said.

Kane shook his head. "Then I really feel sorry for you."

At that moment, Stacy was feeling pretty darned sorry for herself, too. She didn't have to bother to work up some perky spin for Kane, though. This time, he had walked away.

"Be a jerk," she muttered. And when she turned back toward the hauler for that much needed moment of peace and quiet, she saw Nathan watching her. Fair's fair, she supposed.

"Everything okay?" asked Nathan, who was now alone, as she neared.

Apparently, she hadn't been one hundred percent

successful in hiding her conflict with Kane. Heck, with all the people out here, she would have been blessed to have been ten percent successful.

"The crew's good to go," Stacy replied, intentionally misunderstanding his question.

"I don't know about you, but I could use a break," Nathan said. "Want to come inside and sit down?"

"Great minds and all that…the hauler had been my plan, too," she replied.

They walked through the hauler's tool area, where a few of the team members were hanging out, and then into the walled-off lounge area in the front. Stacy was surprised to see that no one else was in there.

Nathan closed the door while Stacy settled in one of the big leather recliners.

"It's been one heck of an evening and the race hasn't even started," Nathan said, as he kicked back in the chair next to hers. "Just in case a dozen people haven't already told you, that was New York Police Detective Lucas Haines giving me a hard time."

"One or two folks might have mentioned it."

As she'd hoped, he smiled at the dry tone of her voice.

Nathan leaned back and tipped his head toward the hauler's ceiling. "He thinks I killed my dad. It's such a sick thought that sometimes I just avoid thinking about it at all. But bottom line is if I can't locate the waitress I was talking to around the time Dad was killed, Haines is going to keep upping the pressure."

"I'm sure he has other suspects, too," Stacy said, though she knew it was scant comfort.

"I'm sure he has a list, but until he crosses me off,

he's wasting valuable time…and making what's already a miserable situation for me worse, yet."

"I'm sorry," Stacy said. "I know this must be awful for you."

Nathan turned his gaze on her. "But for all the awful stuff, I've had some true good come into my life, too."

She knew he was referring to her. "Thank you. The feeling is mutual. You know that, right?"

He gave her a slow and sexy smile. "My memory could always use a little refreshing."

Oh, how very much she wanted to kiss him. And how very much she wanted to unburden herself about her troubles with Kane. She knew she could trust Nathan with all of her heart. Since the kiss would have to wait, she would give him that other form of intimacy…her secret.

"We'll see about that memory refreshing later. Right now—"

Just then, Nathan's cell phone rang. He muttered something under his breath as he pulled the phone from his pocket and then answered it.

"Hi, Maria," Stacy heard him say.

She turned her attention to the television, where prerace programming lit the screen. While she tried to concentrate on an interview with Kent that had been filmed earlier, she couldn't tune out Nathan. It sounded as though something had gone wrong with his business back in Boston…one of their employees leaving, or something. When he'd finished with the call, he looked plain weary.

"Sometimes I don't think I'll make it home soon enough," he said.

Home.

She'd been so carefully avoiding the thought of someplace other than here being where Nathan belonged.

"What's going on?" she asked.

"One of our better employees left. He's someone I should have already asked to join me as a partner, and if I do, maybe he'll come back. I'm gun-shy, though. My last partner ripped me off. I've been working on the assumption that it's easier to do it all by myself than to trust again, but I don't know…. Either way, I've got to come up with an exit plan for this job. I need to be back to Boston, and soon."

Okay, this was when it stank to love someone who only very much liked you. Stacy was sure that he had no idea how much it hurt for her to hear about him leaving, but all the same she wished he'd stop.

And just because she was feeling a little snippy, she said in the honey-sweetest tone possible, "Want me to come help pack your bags?"

The startled look he gave her was another memory for her scrapbook. She just wished like heck that she wouldn't have to rely on that scrapbook so very soon.

"I'm pretty sure I'll be able to handle my bags when the time comes," Nathan replied. "But weren't you about to say something when that call came in?"

"Nothing important," Stacy said. At least nothing important she wanted to share with someone who was already mentally packing his bags.

CHAPTER TWELVE

LIFE SHOULD ALWAYS be like this, Nathan thought as he and Stacy sat in comfortable silence on their way back to her house after the all-star race. Kent had come in third, and while the win didn't bring points with it, the finish had felt good. Stacy's over-the-wall crew had performed as though possessed on their pit stops and dropped a full second. She'd been nearly ecstatic when the times were computed, but she'd told her team she'd known all along that they could do it. That made one of her. Everybody else—Perry and Harley included—had been floored.

"Turn left ahead," Stacy murmured.

"Don't worry, I've got a decent sense of direction," Nathan said. And every cell in his body was leading him Stacy's way at this moment.

They pulled into the lot in front of her town house, and Nathan found a spot next to her car.

"It's good that we have the next two days off," Stacy said. "I need to catch up on laundry and life."

He wished he could have offered her a more exciting alternative, but he knew that tomorrow he'd be working on Liberty Partners business. Nathan turned off the car, exited and came around to open Stacy's door. Once he'd helped her out, he kept his fingers woven between hers. Old-fashioned streetlights sitting in the narrow strip of grass out front of the town houses gave an intimate glow to the night.

"Good job today, Coach," he said.

She smiled. "I had the easy part of the job. No fifty-four-pound tires or eighty-one-pound gas cans for me."

"Being a motivator is a different kind of heavy lifting, and from what I saw, you were darned good at it."

She hesitated a moment before speaking. "I did do well, didn't I?"

It seemed she was beginning to grasp her own worth, and it gave her a glow that was almost incandescent. Without thought, without volition, Nathan pulled Stacy closer and kissed her. He'd wanted this since they'd sat together in the hauler and talked. With her slim body leaning into his, she felt small but not weak. Never weak. That was one of the things he found most appealing about her—that she could hold her own in any sort of scrap. That, and the way she relaxed into him, as though she trusted him with her life.

Then a thought hit Nathan as hard as a mallet to the head: *This must be what it feels like to fall in love.*

He kissed her deeply, wanting more…wanting to feed this hunger suddenly burning in him. He might have kissed her until the streetlights turned off and dawn broke, except that he started feeling as though they were being observed.

Nathan eased off on his kiss and shot a glance toward the row of town houses. Yes…there she was. The watcher was an elderly woman, front and center in her window, drapes open and lights on. He could have sworn she'd just waggled her fingers at him.

He left off the kiss entirely and whispered in Stacy's ear, "There's a woman watching us, and she's not being subtle. She's in the window next to your place."

Stacy looked in the direction he'd gestured. The woman waved and gave them a thumbs-up.

"That's Mrs. Lorenzo," Stacy said. "I'm her hobby."

"She has good taste…and you taste good." Nathan kissed her neck and smiled as Stacy shivered—with pleasure, he hoped. "But do you think we could move this show inside?" he asked. To persuade her, he kissed her again, but suddenly it felt as though no one was home. He squeezed her a little, just to be sure. "Hey…still there?"

"More or less," she replied, then seemed to shake off whatever had been distracting her.

"So what do you say? May I come in for just a little while?"

She hesitated, then stepped away.

"I can't," she said. "It just doesn't feel right."

"Right, as in good?" he teased. "I can fix that."

She shook her head. "No, right as in the correct thing to do. It feels wrong."

That word—*wrong*—was the sound of a barrier gate dropping. Of all the words he could think to apply to this moment—*funny, passionate, incomplete*—*wrong* wasn't among them.

"Nathan, I hope you understand…."

"I do," he said, even though all he really understood was the message, not what motivated it. Because he was a logical man, already he was trying to apply context to her words. He'd seen her with Kane Ledger twice. And both times there had been an odd intimacy to their exchanges.

Was it wrong to be with him because she was involved with someone else? The idea that again—as it had been with his partner, Patricks—he'd missed what should have been obvious didn't sit well. At least Stacy had stopped him, if that was the case.

"It's been a long day for both of us," he said. "You might as well go on in before Mrs. Lorenzo's eyes fall out."

"Thank—" she began to say, but Nathan placed one finger over her lips because he didn't think he could take a thank-you just then.

"Good night," he said, and the moments spent watching her walk to that door and close him out were among the most wretched in Nathan's life.

It was well past one in the morning, and still both Stacy's mind and body hummed with an agitation she couldn't shake. She'd fed Beau some choice bits of corn and watched him put them on his hamster wheel and run with them—his favorite hobby. Hazel was fed and content in her tank for one. Stacy was far less content in her home for one. Since the television didn't appeal and she'd read all the books in her home, she pulled her sole photo album out of her dresser drawer, then curled up on her bed.

Eighteen years of youth, and less than twenty pictures to show for it. There were a few school photos from those random times when Brenda had had enough cash to pay for them. Stacy's senior picture, which she'd paid for by working extra hours at the local burger joint, was there. And a few precious candid shots.

One of Brenda's boyfriends had owned an instant camera. No telling which boyfriend, except that he'd been an early one because Kane—all long-haired rebellious adolescence—was in the photos. In Stacy's mind, most of her mother's boyfriends had blended into a composite memory of sorts—one man's nose with another man's laugh, and the noxious scent of a third man's fat cigars. She'd blocked a lot of her childhood and had no intention of dredging up the specifics, past these pictures.

As she gazed at her favorite photo, one in which she sat on her big brother's shoulders and Brenda stood to one side, her face alight with laughter, Stacy considered the effect her mother had had on both of them.

Kane carried an anger that Stacy couldn't believe originated solely from life with their mother. That childhood had to be part of it, though. As for the rest, maybe one day he'd tell her.

Stacy knew that she, too, hadn't escaped her childhood unscathed, but she'd been pretty sure that she was past the worst of it. Until tonight. Under that streetlight, she'd had almost an out-of-body experience. No longer had it been Stacy and Nathan, but Brenda and any one of the men she'd fancied herself in love with. Though the specifics of the men had melded, her mother's needy clinginess around those men had lingered in Stacy's memory. Suddenly, she'd been an echo of her mother, and that had terrified her.

Or had this perception been so sudden?

She craved family, yet she'd never permitted herself

the chance to have one. There had been men before Nathan who'd expressed romantic interest in her, but each time she had shut them down. Seeking out Kane was the greatest emotional risk she'd taken since childhood. For all of her protestations to Kane about not being the same as Brenda, she'd never fully accepted that, herself.

"Pretty sad," she said to the trio in the old photograph. "All these years later and we still haven't gotten back on track."

Stacy closed the photo album, slipped from bed and tucked it away. It was time to take another small step…to fully risk her heart and seek happiness. Much as she loved Beau and Hazel, they clearly weren't cutting it.

So what about Nathan? If she was going to be totally honest with herself—and tonight seemed to be the night for it—she'd have to admit that it wasn't just a fear of being Brenda that had stopped her from letting Nathan in. If he were staying in the area, she'd say that he was The One, but he would soon be gone, and she didn't see herself leaving with him.

She'd worked too hard for what she had to start again in a new city. She was sure that Boston was a wonderful place, but she could not see herself under Nathan's roof while reestablishing her life. Living upon a wealthy man's good graces simply wasn't her approach to life.

Stacy felt agitated and unready for sleep. Since the alternatives to sleeping were nibbling on the leftovers in her fridge or checking her e-mail, and she wasn't really hungry—just a tad freaked-out—she went to her computer.

First, she checked news sites to read coverage of the night's race. While she hadn't been part of No. 414's over-the-wall pit crew, she felt as proud as if she had been while reading of their challenge win. After reading and rereading everything about the crew that she could find, Stacy checked her e-mail. At the top of the list was one from Kane. The subject line read Sorry, so she figured she could open it in peace.

Stacy smiled at the note's minimal contents. I can be an ass, Kane had written. Not the most eloquent peace offering from a smooth-talking law school graduate, but she'd take it. She hit the reply button and then sent an apology of her own: It must be genetic, since I can be one, too.

Rumor had it that siblings squabbled and siblings made up. Maybe she and Kane were on the right path, after all....

EARLY TUESDAY, Stacy was set to start down another path—her morning run—but it seemed that this one she might be traveling alone. Though she'd seen Nathan's car in the lot, he was nowhere in sight. Instead of beginning with her stretches, Stacy decided to lounge a bit and wait for him.

After using her hand to wipe the cool morning dew off the bench beneath the magnolia tree, Stacy sat, closed her eyes and thought about what most occupied her mind these days—Nathan. Though it didn't stand the test of logic and didn't say much for her resolve, she'd missed him. Silly little events brought him to mind, like Mrs. L doing a cha-cha dance in her window, no doubt as a tribute to Stacy's revved-up love life. And it was love, even if it was short-term, at best.

Suddenly, almost as if she'd wished him there, Stacy heard Nathan say good-morning. She slowly opened her eyes and felt a slight pang of disappointment. He already wore his work clothes.

"A little overdressed for a run, aren't you?" she asked.

"I've got an early meeting, so I'm going to have to pass on the run. I'd like a few minutes of your time, though."

"Okay," she said, then patted the bench right next to where she sat. "Have a seat." Her hand came away damp with dew. "Oops…you'd better not."

She expected some sort of joking comment in return, but Nathan stood silent. Stacy looked closer at his expression; it wasn't exactly love and roses.

"What's up?" she asked.

"I want to talk to you about Saturday night."

"What about it?" she asked, mostly to stall for time. She darned well knew that he wondered why she'd left him standing by the curb.

"How it ended, mostly." For a moment he gazed past her. "Stacy, you know I work hard to be an honorable man, right?"

"Yes." His downright decency was one of the many reasons she'd fallen in love with him.

"And you know I'd never do anything to hurt you?"

She hesitated. This was a bit stickier an issue. "Not intentionally, at least."

"Not quite the answer I'd hoped for, but I'll take it. Knowing all that, there's one thing I need you to be clear on. When I asked to come inside on Saturday, it wasn't because I planned to march straight to your bedroom."

Okay, so maybe only her mind had been going that way. But before she'd freaked out, she'd known that he had wanted her. She'd felt it as much as she'd felt her own need for him.

"But it was on your agenda, right?"

"Yes, but only when you're ready. I'm thirty-one years old, not some randy seventeen-year-old. I'm capable of waiting." He paused, then smiled. "And I know that when the time is right, it will have been worth the wait."

Jeez! And she was twenty-six, but here she was still blushing like a thirteen-year-old. She looked down at her hands folded in her lap because she didn't think she could continue to meet his hot gaze without going up in flames.

"Stacy, I'm going to ask you a question, and I think at this point, it's something I'm entitled to know. Are you dating anybody else?"

Stacy's head shot up. *"What?"*

"It's a fair question…and one you can ask me."

She smiled. "I don't need to ask you because I asked Maria days ago."

His laugh broke some of the tension that still simmered between them. "Figures."

"Honestly, I'm not so sure that I'm even dating you," she said. "We've had one dinner alone, one with the Grosso family, and a lot of runs. Does that constitute dating?"

Nathan took her hands and pulled her to her feet. "It's close enough, considering we're in the middle of NASCAR season."

"Fair enough," Stacy said, keeping her hands clasped in his.

"So," he said. "Dinner tonight? I'll pick you up at your house at eight, and have you home by ten. I will kiss you in front of your snoopy neighbor, walk you to your doorstep, and make sure you get safely into your home…alone. And there you have the full agenda."

Stacy let go of his hands, went up on tiptoe and gave him a quick kiss.

"Good agenda. Gotta run," she said, then did just that.

"Be warned. I'm taking that as a yes," Nathan called after her.

Now if she could just find the courage to give him the other *yes* that came with a full gift of her heart.

CHAPTER THIRTEEN

SMALL STEPS were better than none at all, Nathan told himself on Wednesday morning. In small step number one, he had renegotiated Liberty Partners' recently departed employee back into the fold and promoted him to partner. Clark was bright and honest. In time he'd be able to take his full share of the load, leaving Nathan only his. While this wasn't much in the way of immediate relief, it meant that he could focus his attention elsewhere. Not that it had been far from Stacy, recently.

In yet another small step, the two of them were coming closer to acting like a real couple. They had been out to dinner on Tuesday night, and tonight he was cooking for her at his house. Actually, the housekeeper was going to prepare a meal that he could reheat, which was as close as Nathan got to a stove. Dinner would be safer for all involved that way. But first he had to get through a long day's work.

Maria appeared in the office doorway.

"Just giving you a storm warning. Stacy and Harley are heading this way."

"Any word from the early warning system on what's happening?"

"Nope," she replied in a cheery tone. Sometimes he

suspected that Maria liked to see him suffer just a little. He took it since he knew he'd made her suffer a lot with this North Carolina move.

"Thanks," he said, then put aside the file he'd been working on in order to brace himself for the foul weather ahead.

Stacy was first in the office. Slashes of pink painted her cheekbones, and her hands were neatly closed into fists. Harley followed behind at a more leisurely pace, what Nathan would describe as a bulky—and slightly smug—man's amble.

"Harley has switched Smitty and Stephens," Stacy said. "We're finally getting somewhere and he does this!"

It did seem curious that Harley had made a move. Of course, it was equally curious that Stacy would come storming to him over it. Since it directly pertained to race day, this matter was as out of his domain as it was hers.

"So, you've made this switch?" Nathan asked Harley. "What motivated it?"

Harley took his time settling into a chair before answering. "Twice now, Stephens has been messy with the gas can trade-off. It was horrible at Richmond and a little better on Saturday, but until he gets the kinks worked out, he's better as catch can."

On the surface, Harley's decision made some sense, though Nathan didn't like how pleased the older man was that he'd gotten to upset Stacy in the bargain. Still, Nathan's options were limited. The best he could do was separate the combatants until Stacy cooled down.

"It's your call, Harley," he said. "I'm sure you consulted with Perry?"

Harley nodded. "He agrees it's worth a shot."

"Okay, thanks," he said to Harley. "Unless you've got something to add, I don't know if there's much reason for you to stick around here."

"As I told you in the first place," Harley said to Stacy.

Instead of answering, she walked to the windows and looked out. After Harley had left, she turned back and again planted herself in front of his desk, in what he considered a pretty aggressive stance for such a usually peaceable woman.

"I was upset before I came in, but now…now I don't think a month at a yoga retreat would get my blood pressure down. You just left me there to twist in the wind in front of *that man!*" she cried.

"Care to have a seat?" Nathan asked.

"No."

"*That man* has the right to consult with Perry and make crew changes," he pointed out, "A few weeks ago, you stood in this office and agreed to just that."

"That was before I realized that Harley Mickowski has a nasty vindictive streak."

Though he might tone down the rhetoric, Nathan couldn't argue that one. He didn't have to, though. "Stacy, he gave a sound enough reason for what he's doing."

"Look at the tapes from last week! Stephens might have hesitated a millisecond."

"But it was perceptible?"

"Yes," she admitted. "Still, it's crazy to move him when he's on an upswing."

"Yet within the realm of acceptable business judgment. Now tell me why this has you so angry?"

"I'll never be able to prove it, but I feel as though he did this as a way to make me fail."

"That's a pretty strong accusation, don't you think?" Nathan asked. He could see that she was angry and running on emotion, not thought.

"Okay, so maybe I was a little crazy to promise a ten percent time drop," she said, continuing as though he hadn't spoken at all. "It was totally my fault for offering that, but I didn't know how else to make you relate. And now, when I'm actually coming close to pulling off a miracle, Harley does this?" She flung her hands outward in a gesture of absolute frustration. "How should I feel?"

"Upset? Challenged?"

"Yes to both of the above. And trapped and conned."

"Okay, but as ill-tempered as Harley can be, do you think he'd actually do anything to harm the team?"

"Yes," she said flatly.

He didn't argue. Instead, he watched as Stacy struggled to reconcile what she was feeling with logic. He knew that eventually she'd come out in the right place. She was both too smart and too inherently fair to have it happen any other way.

"Okay, probably not," she admitted. "Except he really, *really* wants me gone. What better way to do it than to up the ante by moving the guys around?"

"That's one viewpoint," he said.

"But not yours."

"No. But what is it you want from me?"

"I wanted you to tell him that he can't pull that garbage."

"Even if I agreed with you, you know that would be

out of my control, as much as it is out of yours. I suppose you could go talk to Perry, Dean and Patsy, but I strongly advise against it. So long as Harley can support his decision, they're going to go with it. What's your fall-back position?"

She looked startled. "How did you know that I have one?"

"Because you're too smart not to."

She looked pleased at his response, but still far from pacified.

"Okay, here's my fall-back," she said. "I don't feel that I should be penalized for what could be a disastrous decision. If the times are worse this weekend, I don't want them to count against me."

"And if it was a brilliant decision and they're better?"

"I use them, of course."

He leaned back in his chair and tried to relax a little. He didn't like arguing, and especially not with Stacy. "Don't you see something a little lopsided in that scenario?"

"So long as it's in my favor, I don't care."

He had to smile at that one. "Picking and choosing times wasn't part of the deal."

The smile she gave him was sexy…intimate. "So we can renegotiate."

"Now you're using our relationship as leverage. Is that fair to either of us? And is that the way you want to step into this job?"

"First, I wasn't trying to leverage anything. Whatever you think I just did is a problem with your perception, not my behavior. Second, I want the job, and I don't want to lose it because of a decision I had no control over."

"Stacy, you know as well as I do that, ultimately, this is a team. Once a decision is made, everyone on the team has to stand behind it, regardless of personal misgivings. If you can't accept that, maybe this isn't the place for you, after all."

"You're making sure it's not my place. You know, suddenly you're looking a lot like Harley to me."

He'd angered her, he knew. But he'd had no choice. "I'm just reminding you of the realities of working in a team atmosphere."

"Thanks, but I'm well aware of them."

He didn't hear a whole lot of actual gratitude in her tone.

"Look, this is business. It isn't personal. I know you're upset with me, but you need to put this in its proper perspective."

"Just tell me what my choices are," she said.

"The best I can see it, you have one choice…to go back out there and work with Stephens and Smitty until they have this change down."

"So you're counting the times on Saturday?"

"Whether faster or slower, yes."

She shook her head. "I didn't expect this of you."

"And I didn't expect *this* of you, either," he replied.

Hands on hips, she stood there examining him as though he were some sort of museum display…probably male *Homo sapiens stupidius*.

"I think I'll skip dinner tonight, and work late, if you don't mind," she finally said.

Since he wasn't one hundred percent sure that she wouldn't have slipped a little something nasty into his food, Nathan was all for it.

"Do what you have to do," he said. "And when you come to see that this wasn't personal, let me know."

"I'll be sure to drop you a line," she said then turned heel. Once framed by the doorway, she added, "You live in Boston, right?"

That last dart definitely hit its mark.

THAT EVENING as Stacy drove home, she went through a mental checklist of reasons her day might possibly have spun out of control in such a full-fledged crazy way. It wasn't, to her knowledge, a full moon. No big storm approached, and from an astrological point of view, she was pretty sure that Mercury wasn't in retrograde. However, she planned to go inside and remain in peace and solitude until morning...just in case.

Make that peace and solitude right after she gave someone what-for for taking her assigned resident parking spot. She pulled into a nearby guest spot and walked toward the low-slung Porsche to see what sort of high-and-mighty was visiting her modest neck of the woods...and poaching on her parking spot.

The driver's door opened, and Stacy wouldn't have been any more surprised to see a rock star than she was her brother exit the car.

"Hello, Kane," she said. "I'd ask what brings you here, but I figure the answer is me."

"You'd be right," he responded after he'd closed the car door. "I think it's time that we talked, and I didn't want it to be around your work or mine."

Kane, who was usually so cool and direct, sounded almost nervous. This was something she never thought she'd hear.

"Okay." She glanced up at the building and caught Mrs. L moving in front of her window, no doubt to catch the show.

"Would you like to come inside?" she asked her brother.

"No, thanks. Let's just get this done."

"You make talking sound like a root canal," she said, trying to tease him into a little lightness.

"I'm looking at it more like cauterizing a wound."

"That doesn't sound too swell, either," she replied.

"Swell." He shook his head. "Now there's a word…one that definitely doesn't apply to this situation." He looked up as the streetlights above them switched on. "Stacy, I need to tell you something, and then you can decide if you still want to have me around."

"Okay. Are you sure you don't want to come inside?" she asked again. When he said no, she made a shooing motion at Mrs. L, who actually complied. Stacy wasn't sure how long the good behavior would stick—hopefully long enough for Kane to say his piece.

"Do you remember the day I left home?" he asked her.

"Not really, but keep in mind I was only five. Beyond that, I've blocked a lot."

"I don't blame you," Kane muttered. "I'm going to tell you what I remember."

"Okay," she said, even though she wasn't certain she wanted to hear this.

"Do you remember begging me to take you along?" he asked.

She smiled. Though it was a sad thought, it was

something she could see herself doing. "No, but I'm not surprised."

"Well, you did. Actually, first you demanded, and then when I told you I couldn't, you begged. Finally, you wrapped your arms around one of my legs and refused to let go."

"Very Ghandi-esque of me," she said. "There's nothing like a little passive resistance."

"I'm glad you can joke about it," he said in a tight voice.

"Hey, it was a long time ago. And besides, if you don't see humor in the bad times, that doesn't leave a whole lot to take forward in life, does it?"

He shrugged. "I guess that's why I look forward more than back. That, and guilt."

"Guilt?"

"The night I left, Brenda had to peel you off of me. Brenda and I started yelling at each other. She told me that I had to stay. That if I bailed out on the two of you, I was as bad as my old man. Her boyfriend, Chuck—"

The name brought back a memory. "Hey, did he smoke big cigars?"

"Yes," Kane said.

Stacy shuddered. "I remember him. I've hated the smell of cigars since childhood."

"You should. He was there. You started crying and wouldn't stop, so Chuck smacked you across the back of your head. I couldn't stand it. I jumped Chuck, broke his nose, and would have happily killed him, but Brenda called the police on me. I took off, and the last thing I heard before I left that pit of an apartment was you crying and screaming my name."

It was almost as though she were looking at a photo album. Maybe she remembered the event, but maybe she was just reliving Kane's depiction. Either way, the fright and the hurt washed through her again. This time, though, she was a grown woman and could put the event in perspective.

"Okay, so that sucks," she said. "Small wonder I blocked it. But as I said, it was a long time ago, Kane."

He looked down at the ground and then back at her. "I should have taken you with me, Stacy. I can't believe I left you there in that hell."

There were plenty of times in her childhood that Stacy had thought the exact same thing. But later, when she'd been old enough to understand the workings of the world, she had let her anger go.

"Hang on, there," she said. "You were seventeen. What were you going to do with me, assuming that you could have legally taken me? It doesn't sound as though you had a plan."

"I don't know what I would have done…found us a room in a boardinghouse, worked a few years more before starting college." He ran a hand though his hair, leaving it looking as rough as she was beginning to feel. "All I know is that I could have made it work, and that from that day, I've felt like garbage for leaving you. Oh, don't get me wrong," he said, then gave her a bitter smile. "I moved on, probably far more easily than I should have. And then, when you started trying to get back in touch with me, I pretended that you didn't exist. Better that than face what I had done."

"Well, *that* ticked me off," she said. "I'm not much for being ignored."

He nearly smiled. "I'll bet you're not."

"But going back to ancient times, you did what you had to. I don't remember much, but I do remember you and Mom fighting a lot. It wasn't good there, that's for sure. And beyond that, if you'd stayed in Halesboro, you wouldn't be where you are today. You should be proud of yourself," she said fiercely. "I've *always* been proud of you."

"You shouldn't be. You want to know the very worst of it? And this is what really kills me…. I didn't leave to better myself. I left because of a girl. She'd used me and dumped me, and I was so stupid and angry and bitter that I went and dumped you."

"Okay, so your reasons for leaving weren't exactly noble. So what? How long do you plan to torture yourself over this?"

"Indefinitely seems to be the answer."

For a guy who, on the surface, appeared to have it all together, Kane sure had his issues. Suddenly, she felt much more a big sister than a little one.

"You know, you really need to get over yourself and let it go," she said.

Kane's choked sound of disbelief was one for her memory book, for sure, but he needed to hear a few basic truths. She expected that too many people held back with him because he was so good at putting them off.

"I'm willing to forgive you for things you did when you were seventeen, but now you're—what?—thirty-eight, and my patience is pretty much tapped out," she said. "If you're going to go all mean and tragic on me every time you see me, how is that moving forward? And to the extent you feel you need to atone—which I don't think you do at all, but hey, that's just little me—how is it atonement to treat me poorly?"

"It's not." He tilted his head and regarded her carefully. Stacy felt uncomfortable under all that attention. "You should have been the lawyer in the family," he said. "That was one sharp analysis…one I totally missed."

"You're too fond of the subject…*you*."

He laughed. "I've missed a lot, not having you in my life."

She smiled, but mostly to mask the tears she felt welling. "I like to think so."

"So, do you forgive me?" he asked.

"I still don't think you did anything all those years ago that requires forgiveness, but if that's what it takes to get you back on track, consider yourself forgiven," she said. "Now, do you suppose that maybe I could have the first contact I've had with you since Brenda peeled me off your leg?"

He drew her into his arms and gave her a hug…the sort of squeeze-the-breath-from-a-girl type hug she'd craved for so very long. She hugged him back with all the love she'd stored up. Before her inevitable—and well-earned—tears started, she tried to stave them off with humor. "Now, about your more recent behavior, big brother…I think a month spent driving that car of yours would just about make up for the grief."

"A week," he replied. Though he was trying to joke along, too, she could hear the raw emotion in his voice.

"Done," she decreed. And despite the sound of a car pulling in, she gave her brother one last, long hug.

Finally, the drought was over.

CHAPTER FOURTEEN

NATHAN CONSIDERED himself the possessor of a re-
markably efficient and rational brain. Usually in less than
a heartbeat he could fully analyze the consequences of any
move he planned to make. But at that moment, it seemed
his rational brain had been incinerated by the heat of anger.
The rest of him was soon to follow, and for good reason.

He had been lied to and cheated on yet again!

He'd been smart to have been gun-shy after Tom
Patricks, but not quite smart enough. If he had carried
the lesson over into his personal life, he would have
saved himself this pain. Sucker that he was, he'd come
here tonight to apologize to Stacy for his bluntness over
the conflict at work, to let her know that he loved her,
and that no matter what happened at Cargill-Grosso,
that would always be true.

"Idiot," Nathan berated himself. "Total idiot."

Stacy had told him that she wasn't seeing anyone
else. Yet there she was, clearly wrapped in Kane
Ledger's arms. The bitterness washing over him was a
physical thing, tasting sharp and ugly in his mouth.

He shouldn't be surprised at the betrayal. He'd seen
them together before. Somewhere in his subconscious,
the thought had been simmering that if there was

nothing but business of some sort between Stacy and Kane, he would have heard her mention Ledger.

Then, another sickening realization hit him. Now that Nathan thought about it, she'd never actually said that she *wasn't* seeing anyone else. She'd turned the question around to whether *they* were truly dating. So maybe she hadn't lied, but she'd played him for the fool that he'd been.

Nathan pulled into an open spot nearly in front of the couple. Close enough, at least, that they were lit by his car's headlight beams as though they were onstage. They had pulled away from each other, and Stacy had cupped her hand over her eyes, trying to see who was in the car. She needn't have made the effort.

Nathan didn't bother with basics like turning off his car and taking the keys. He just smacked it into Neutral, pulled the parking break and jumped out, intent on doing…doing *what?* It was too early for swords or pistols at dawn, and yet here he was, feet away from them, and steaming furious.

"Hello, Nathan," Kane said. "I didn't expect to see you here."

"Obviously not," Nathan replied, but kept his attention focused on Stacy. In the glare of the headlights, she looked confused, bemused, maybe even a little amused. But definitely not guilty. He wanted guilt from her, and a heavy dose of remorse. He wanted her to at least acknowledge that she'd done wrong.

"Incredible," Nathan said. "You know, I've always thought myself a pretty smart guy…not the smartest out there, but plenty smart to have sniffed this out. And yet you fooled me."

"Fooled you, how?" Kane asked.

"Keep out of this, Ledger," Nathan demanded. "I'm dealing with Stacy, and only Stacy. How long have the two of you had something going on?" he asked her.

"Going on?" she echoed.

"How long have you been involved?" He'd stretched out that last word long and low, to cover the multitude of activities that were spinning through his mind.

"In—" she began to say, but then covered her face with her hands and made a sound that might have been a laugh, but just as easily could have been a cry. She dropped her hands, walked two steps toward him, started to say something else, then spun away.

"Stacy, it's going to be okay," Kane said in a calming voice, one that Nathan imagined he used to talk clients back from a precipice.

But what did Stacy have to be upset over, other than having been caught?

Already, Nathan's rational brain was beginning a phoenixlike rise from its ashes. *Something's looking a little off, here, pal,* it was saying.

"How long have we been involved?" Stacy repeated. "Kane and I have been involved since birth!"

You're toast, Rational Brain decreed.

In that instant, it all came back to him—that night when Stacy had been on the treadmill, running for all she was worth and announcing that she had an estranged brother…the fact that he'd never seen any sort of tension other than anger between Stacy and Kane… and the fact that the hug he'd just witnessed had been far from passionate.

Nathan hazarded a look Kane's way. The guy's expression only reinforced the toast theory.

"Stacy is my sister," Ledger said. "Actually, half sister, if we're going to get technical about it."

"No need to get technical," Nathan replied. The only real need he could sense was for him to start apologizing, and quickly.

He took a step toward Stacy.

"No closer," she decreed in an eerily emotionless tone.

"I'm sorry," he said.

"And I'm sorry I let you past walls I never should have, but not again."

"Look," he said. "It was a stupid but honest mistake."

She kept on going as if he hadn't spoken. "Here is what I want from you…nothing. I want you to leave my home and neighborhood and not come back. Obviously, we have to continue a work relationship, but I don't want a word from you outside of business. Not even talk of the weather, please."

"Stacy, I know you're angry, but I want you to think about this. You have to understand how I might have thought that you and…well, thought what I did," he finished saying, figuring there was no point in voicing his idiot assumption twice.

"Apparently, somewhere along the line you decided that maybe because I'm not as well educated as you or as sophisticated as you, that also means I lack morals. I can handle people thinking I'm a fluffy blonde. I can tolerate people sometimes talking down to me, but I cannot and will not deal with people who think that I'm the sort of woman who would lead on a man."

She stalked closer, but Nathan didn't retreat. He'd take his verbal blows because he'd earned them.

"I would never lie," she said. "I would never manipulate you. That even for a second you could think that of me…I thought I…"

He could hear the tears in her voice before he saw the evidence of them on her face, and he hated having been the cause. He held out his hand to her.

"Stacy…"

"No!" She backed away, wiping at her tears. "I thought that you and I…" She shook her head. "I believed…" And then she fled to her front door.

The moments that she fumbled with her key before she could get inside felt endless to Nathan. He wanted to go help her but knew that, too, would never be forgiven. Once her door had slammed, he looked toward Mrs. L's window, half-expecting her mocking applause. But even Mrs. L had turned her back on him tonight, and Nathan knew he deserved no less.

Kane Ledger's dry voice cut into Nathan's self-inflicted misery.

"That goes down in the annals of massive screwups," Stacy's brother said.

"Tell me something I don't know," Nathan replied sarcastically. Of course, then he realized there were probably a great many things that Ledger *could* tell him.

"I think I've had enough high drama for one night," Kane said, before turning to leave.

"Hang on," Nathan said, then softened the order to a request with a "please."

"What?"

"Just tell me…if you can…why Stacy reacted like she did? It was an honest mistake on my part, the kind of thing we all could have laughed off."

"Except no one was laughing," Kane pointed out.

"Exactly. Why the overreaction on Stacy's part?"

Ledger drew a slow hiss of air between his teeth. "A piece of advice, man to man. Should Stacy ever unbend enough to speak to you, I'd leave the word overreaction out of your groveling, okay?"

"Good general advice, but I think you've got some specific reasons to back that up, don't you?"

Kane shrugged. "If Stacy wants to tell you, that's her business. It's none of mine."

"Look, I'm asking you to throw me a bone. The last thing I want to do—now or in the future—is hurt your sister."

"Sounds like a good starting point," Kane agreed.

"So tell me how to avoid stepping in it all over again."

Kane hesitated before speaking. "Has Stacy ever mentioned a woman named Brenda?"

"Brenda? No."

"She was our mother. Is, I suppose…" He looked at his watch and gave a semiannoyed sigh. "This is going to take some time. How about another day?"

"How about now? There's a pub down the street, and I'm a fast listener," Nathan offered.

He stood silent while Kane debated the suggestion.

"Might as well get it out of the way, as long as I've devoted tonight to cleaning up messes," Ledger said.

Nathan didn't know what else the guy had been dealing with, but he couldn't dispute the tag of mess when applied to him.

"Thanks," he said to Kane. "I'll owe you."

Ledger's laugh was as dry as his sense of humor. "Trust me, I'll collect…or my sister will for me."

"INTO EACH PERSON'S LIFE some rain must fall, so where the heck is the literal stuff?" Stacy asked the heavens forty-seven laps into a miserable race in Charlotte the following Sunday.

The over-the-wall pit crew had tanked on the sole pit stop thus far, gaining over three-quarters of a second. The skies were a sullen gray, so heavy with rain that Stacy felt that Mother Nature was spiting her by withholding it. At this point, a rain-shortened race was her best bet not to have the guys add more time to their average.

She knew that this week she was as much to blame as Harley's switch of Stephens and Smitty, which he was sorely regretting already. Since Wednesday, she'd tried her hardest not to let her broken heart bleed over into her work life, but it was darned tough with Nathan always lingering just on the outskirts of her daily activities. Though he'd sent beautiful flowers with a note of apology to her home, at least he'd honored her request at work and stayed away. She knew he was sorry, but that wouldn't rebuild what he'd destroyed.

The race ended not in the downpour that Stacy had wanted, but in one decent pit stop that had shaved off a few tenths of what they had gained in time, and then a splash 'n go, where just fuel was added, and which, technically, shouldn't be counted toward her promised time drop.

One by one, the crew came to talk to her. Smitty was the last.

"Sorry, Coach," he said. "I tried."

"I know you did," Stacy replied. "All of you did, but we were just off today."

He nodded. "It's like there's been something in the air."

My bad vibes, Stacy thought before reminding herself that she wasn't quite the center of the universe. All the same, she needed to get over Nathan, and somehow accomplish that in even less time than it had taken to fall in love with him.

Minutes later, she had to put her resolution to the test; Nathan stopped by as she was packing up the last of her meager gear. Stacy put on her best business face, only to have it slip a bit when Kane arrived, too. She'd talked to him daily since Black Wednesday, as she'd tagged it.

The best thing about Kane was that he thought like a guy. Obviously. She could do many things, but that miracle—or was it a curse?—she couldn't pull off. Kane gave her insight, sometimes of the unwelcome variety.

"Hello, Stacy…Kane…" Nathan said, looking a little frustrated at Kane's arrival. "So, how did the pit crew do?"

She'd already seen him talking to Harley so he darned well knew it hadn't been a good show. But she had said she'd talk business, so business she would talk.

"Although we worked hard this week to deal with the changes we faced, I'm sure you noticed that pit stop times were up. I don't have the final numbers, but it's looking like an overall increase of two-tenths on a full stop. I'm not including the splash 'n go in my numbers, as I'm sure you wouldn't allow that anyway."

"Stacy—"

She shook her head in a very firm no. No, she didn't want to hear the regret in his voice, and no, she would not love him anymore…no matter what her traitorous heart was clamoring for her to do.

"I know you're counting these times against me," she said. "You made that very clear last week, and I won't bring up the topic again. I'll be sure to drop a report on the final times with Maria. Is there anything else you want?" she asked, with an "I dare you" challenge in her tone.

And even if Kane hadn't been giving Nathan a subtle shake of his head best interpreted as "don't go there," Stacy knew he wouldn't have. He might have misjudged her horribly, but she knew that he remained at his core a gentleman.

"There's nothing else. Thank you," Nathan said, and then left.

"You might consider giving the guy a slight break," Kane suggested once Nathan was out of earshot.

"Not a chance."

"Why not?"

"Because I learned how to cry again on Wednesday night, and then it took me three days to stop. If I let down my guard and he hurts me again, there's no telling how long it will take me to get over it."

Kane held up a warning hand. "Okay, too much emotion for my comfort level. You could just tell me to butt out?"

He'd sounded so hopeful that Stacy had to smile.

"No such luck, bro," she said. "You have years of missed interference to make up for. But I'll try not to rattle you with tears and the like."

She was rattling herself quite enough, already. Out of habit and probably some innate desire to torture herself, she quickly looked around for Nathan. He wasn't far off, just over by the hauler. And he was, of course, looking her way.

Yes, into each person's life, some rain must fall. Now if hers would just wash away the pain of loving Nathan Cargill.

"TODAY IS YOUR lucky day," Hank Overstreet said by way of phone greeting to Nathan on Tuesday morning.

"Good thing. I've been overdue for one," Nathan replied while riffling through piles of correspondence that seemed to have multiplied while he'd been at the track. At this point, he wasn't quite sure if there was a desk beneath it all.

Although Sunday had been a decent day for Cargill-Grosso, it had been miserable for him. After fighting against it for days, Nathan had finally accepted that Stacy wasn't going to give him a chance to make up for his mistake…not now and not ever.

"Elena Cruz is working as a housekeeper at a private residence on Fisher Island, just off Miami. Not a poor choice, considering all the security around those mega-mansions," Overstreet said.

Nathan's heart beat faster. "You've talked to her?"

"Yes, and I'm sure we have the right person. She's agreed to give a statement to the police. Do you have a pen and paper handy?"

"Yes," Nathan said, then quickly jotted the contact information that Hank gave him.

After thanking the private investigator, Nathan

hurried to make another call…one that had been a half a year in the making. Except that Lucas Haines wasn't answering. Three messages on Haines's voice mail, two calls to rather disinterested NYPD secretaries, and one terse "call me" e-mail to Haines later, Nathan had to set aside the idea of instantaneous vindication. Frustration simmered just beneath his skin. Trying to relax, he leaned back in his chair and looked around the office that had been his for far too many months.

"Why am I here?" he asked aloud, and he didn't mean it in an existential way.

His father's legacy was in good hands with the Grossos. He knew that, despite Dean's protestations and procrastination, Nathan was readily replaceable on the business end of the operation. And Stacy Evans wanted nothing to do with him. So what was keeping him here?

Oh, he'd miss the people he'd met, but he could always come back around to visit. He'd miss the rich scent of a North Carolina morning as he ran…but that memory was too interwoven with those of Stacy to be one he'd pull out often. Boston had its own charms, and maybe, eventually, once he was ready, its own women, too.

So what was keeping him here? The same thing that now made him ready to leave. Stacy.

Nathan pushed back from his desk and went to find Dean and Patsy, whom he'd earlier seen in Kent's garage area. After a couple of minutes of searching, he found them outside the gift shop. Dean was signing autographs for a throng of thrilled fans. Patsy stood, as she had for his racing career, far enough away to let the fans have their fill.

"I think he misses this," Patsy said to Nathan. "It's a good thing he can get it out of his system now and then."

Dean glanced over and said, "Do you need us, Nathan?"

"Just for a minute," he confirmed.

After Dean had signed the last of the requested autographs, the three of them walked back toward Kent's garage, which had once been Dean's.

"I wanted you to be the first to know that we've found the woman who's my alibi in my father's murder," Nathan said. "As soon as I can get the information to Lucas Haines and he confirms it, I'll be cleared."

"It's about time," Dean replied.

Nathan nodded his head in agreement. "I've also wanted to thank the two of you for supporting me, but I've never known how to raise the topic without dragging talk back around to Dad's death. All the same, knowing that you stood behind me made this whole mess almost tolerable."

"We wouldn't have had it any other way. We've lived in the public eye a long time, Nathan," Patsy said. "We understand how tough it is, and how cutting the gossip can be, even after you've developed a thick skin."

Nathan slowed, and the Grossos matched his pace. He didn't want to be in the garage or in an office. He wanted to be free, breathing fresh air.

"My skin's thick enough, but this was an experience I don't ever want to repeat. I want to get back to my private life, where the people who think they know me, actually do."

"This is beginning to sound like a resignation speech," Dean said.

Nathan had to admit to a small twinge of regret, but he knew he was doing what was best for both him and Cargill-Grosso.

"It is," he said. "I know that I had agreed to stay…but I don't think that's going to be possible. Without going into too much detail, let's just say that I need to get my life back to where it was. I'd like to be in Boston by the first of July. That will give you a month to find a replacement. I'm sure that in the stack of résumés you both have, there's someone. I'll sit in on the interviews if you want me to, and commute down here to help with any issues the new hire might have this season. But I have to leave."

"I knew I couldn't stall you forever," Dean said. "But we've liked having you around. The continuity has been good."

"And I've liked being around."

Just then, Stacy walked by with a few pit crew members. They surrounded her like a cordon of bodyguards, except that they were laughing at something she'd just said. Her life was parading on very well without him.

"Nathan, are you all right?" Patsy asked, cutting into his thoughts.

He gave one last glance toward Stacy.

"I will be," he said.

Patsy looked Stacy's way. "She's a keeper, I think."

"What are you talking about?" Dean asked his wife.

She gave him the sort of patient smile that more than once Nathan had received from Stacy.

"Don't worry yourself about it, sweetheart," she said to Dean. "Nathan knows what I'm talking about."

He did, but it was far too late to do anything about it. As of July first, if not sooner, he wouldn't even be a spectator in Stacy Evans's life.

CHAPTER FIFTEEN

THE WORKDAYS before the Dover race were both the longest and the shortest that Stacy had ever experienced. Because she knew this might be her last week with the guys, she made a conscious effort to savor each moment, and those moments flew by. As much as she enjoyed being a fitness trainer for her private clients, she enjoyed the team spirit and challenge of the NASCAR world even more, and Cargill-Grosso was the very best place in which to pursue it.

While she hadn't given up on keeping a job with Kent's pit crew—and, in fact, had spent the past three nights working on a proposal to start a fitness program for the entire facility—if she did lose this job, she'd be knocking on the doors of other racing teams. Cargill-Grosso remained her first choice, though, both because she'd miss her guys terribly and because she wanted that college degree. She had worked up the courage to contact the admissions office at UNC Charlotte and was now in the process of lining up her testing date and getting her application together. But while business was shaping up, matters of the heart kept crumbling.

Her morning runs had been solitary. By Thursday, it had become clear that Nathan wasn't going to run so long as she was out there. He'd been polite when he'd seen her, always saying hello, but never giving her an extra word or look. And for that sad reason her days had dragged.

Kane insisted that she was punishing Nathan for a crime he didn't even know existed. Since she hadn't shared the details of her past with Nathan, how could she expect him to know how much his accusations would hurt? Good point, she supposed. Not that it mattered.

Maria had been doing a happy dance all week because the Grossos had started interviewing candidates for Nathan's job; she and Nathan would be back in Boston in time for Independence Day and fireworks over the Charles River. And Stacy would be in uptown Charlotte, watching the celebration that would mark the beginning of yet another year in her life without any fireworks of the romantic sort. She had no intention of dating until totally over Nathan, and he wasn't going to be an easy man to get over.

Now it was race day in Dover, and even with the roar of the fans surrounding her, Stacy felt horribly alone. The drivers had been announced and had returned to their teams. It was time for the prayer and the National Anthem. As she did at each race, Stacy sang along. This time, though, the excitement of the moment wasn't quite the same. In fact, those darned tears were creeping back. As subtly as she could, she wiped one from the corner of her eye. With luck, everyone would think it was the emotion of the moment and not the sadness she fought so hard to shake.

As a formation of military jets flew overhead in

salute to the people below, Stacy looked skyward. While she did, she felt the weight of a gaze upon her. She looked to her left and caught Nathan watching her. Though her love was futile, it existed all the same, and the regret she saw on his face cut her as deeply as her own pain. She tried to give him an "it will all work out" smile, but she couldn't quite pull it off.

Embarrassed, Stacy turned away and focused on the race about to start. She wished the Grossos and Tanya good luck before they left to watch the event from the top of the hauler. She gave her guys one extra round of high fives, and sent some good vibes Perry and Harley's way. And she tried not to think about Nathan.

"Something feels right about today," Calvin said to her as the cars followed the pace car around the track, with Kent taking his tenth position, based on qualifying time.

"We need something to go very, very right," Stacy replied, not bothering to add *since everything is so very, very wrong in my personal life.*

To achieve her bargained upon ten percent time drop, the guys needed to cut a half a second today. The goal was far from impossible, and since she'd done all she could, Stacy knew she needed to relax. To some, that might have been impossible with the noise of the crowd and cars, the scents of burning rubber and spent fuel, and the intense concentration that seemed to make the air thicker down pit road. But for Stacy, it meant that all was right in this part of her world.

Kent must have been feeling some of the magic that Calvin had sensed since he was steadily creeping up through the pack. Soon, though, Perry would be calling him in for fuel and tires. She glanced anxiously at the crew chief to see if he seemed to be near that point. Stacy was so wrapped up in the action that until a hand briefly settled on her arm, she hadn't noticed that someone had come up beside her. Then she'd hardly needed to look to know who it was. The tingle that shot through her told her it was Nathan.

"This is one of the tightest pit roads on the circuit," he said into her ear. "The crew chiefs and spotters really earn their money getting the drivers in and out."

Stacy nodded, but kept staring at the race. She didn't know why he'd decided to approach her, but because she was feeling sad and lonely, she'd take the contact, as fleeting as it was.

Perry signaled Kent, who was hanging tough in fifth place, into pit road. Several other drivers were coming in at the same time, and Stacy could see what Nathan had meant. There was little room for error. Kent's team got him in with all the skill that Stacy had come to expect. Now to see how her guys performed....

Stacy had developed the ability to concentrate on the fine details, even as the crew moved at a superhuman pace. As she watched, she saw nothing that she'd even think of tweaking. Seconds passed as her entire week had—both quickly and slowly at the same time. After the car was down and Kent safely off pit road, she allowed herself to breathe again. And then she checked the time she'd automatically hit on her stopwatch.

"Twelve-one," she said, nearly unable to believe her eyes. That was better than a seven-tenths drop off their current average.

Nathan had somehow materialized next to her again. She showed him the time on the watch.

"Good," he said. "You're edging closer to this job."

"Do you care?" she asked. She didn't mean it in a sarcastic way; she was truly curious.

"I want you to get everything you dream of. That might not include me, but, yes, I still care."

And then he walked away.

As she turned her attention back to the race, all Stacy could think was that she cared, too. Altogether too much.

NATHAN KNEW he was being a sucker, and his purportedly rational brain was cheering him along. Great help that was. Activity hummed around him, and all he could do was watch Stacy. He told himself that he was just trying to drink in these last hours around her, but it was more than that.

Watching and waiting. That's all the past week had been about. He still hadn't heard a word from Lucas Haines, but that had stopped mattering nearly as much as knowing that his time with Stacy was almost at an end. He had watched her from afar all week, and he had hated the distance. He had hated the hours when he didn't see her, and he had begun to rebel at the thought of not seeing her again.

It was love, and it was far from rational, but there was no changing it…even if she couldn't stand him. Except that he knew deep in his bones that she cared about him, too. At least, that's what he hoped.

He had to do something to demolish the wall she'd built around herself all over again. This one was bigger and more daunting…designed for the specific purpose of keeping him out. At least she cared enough to need to push him away, he supposed.

Nathan lost track of the race, focused only on Stacy. When Kent came down pit road again, instead of watching the over-the-wall pit crew, he stared at Stacy watching them and urging them on. Crazy. He remained flat-out crazy…in love.

"Great concentration for a guy with all of your troubles," said a voice from beside him.

Nathan looked away from Stacy long enough to confirm that it was indeed Lucas Haines. He couldn't say that he was happy to see the man—at least not in the normal sense of the word—but he was damned glad.

"I have troubles, but you're not among them," he said to the detective. "Don't you ever return a call?"

"Do you think your father's is the only case I'm handling?"

"You don't want to hear what I think about you, Haines."

"Probably not," the man agreed. "And you already know what I think about you. So where does that leave us?"

Without answering or even looking at the detective again, Nathan walked toward the hauler and its relative quiet. He knew that Haines would follow. There, in the empty space where the toolboxes would again be stored for transport after the race, Nathan pulled his cell phone from his pocket and pushed the speed dial number for Hank Overstreet.

"I've got someone who could use some good, old-fashioned detective training from you," Nathan said to Hank when he answered.

Overstreet's gruff laugh was one of the better sounds that Nathan had heard in a long time.

"Put him on," Hank said.

Nathan held out the phone to Haines. "Hate to spoil your day, but I've got my alibi."

"Or so you say," Haines said, then took the phone.

Nathan let satisfaction seep into his bones as he watched Haines's frantic note-scratching followed by a few more minutes of calls from his own cell phone.

"You're in the clear," Haines said, once he'd hung up.

"I always was," Nathan replied. "Now that you know, I hope this wasn't a wasted trip for you."

Haines shrugged. "You've never been the only suspect. I've got other reasons to be around here."

Nathan laughed, and for the first time since he and Stacy had experienced their blowup, it was a real laugh…with real joy.

"I've got other reasons to be around here, too," he said to the detective, then held out his hand as a peace offering. "I know you were just doing your job."

"I'll find the killer," Haines said, and shook Nathan's hand.

"I've never doubted that," Nathan replied. "Keep me up-to-date, would you?"

"Of course. And I really am sorry for your loss."

"Thank you." Nathan released the detective's hand and headed toward the hauler's door. "Now, if you don't mind, I think I'll get on with my life."

Scant seconds later, Nathan was back by the pit wall, watching the one person he wanted to be an intimate part of that life.

"How did they do?" he asked Stacy, referring to the pit stop he'd missed.

"Good," Stacy said.

"When this is all over, can we talk?" he asked.

"Why? What do we have to talk about?"

He'd never thought this was going to be easy. "I think you know."

"All I know is that I need to work, and that you're messing with my concentration," she said over the noise around them.

Neither a yes nor a no… Nathan decided he could live with that for now.

He moved back from the cluster of team members closest to the pit wall. He didn't want to distract her, but he didn't want her out of his sight, either. He'd barely stepped away when a loud, cracking noise split the humid air. Two cars had veered together right in front of Kent's pit stall. Frozen in place, he watched as one got nudged all the way into the wall.

People scattered.

Nathan looked for only one person in the commotion…the one who had claimed his heart. And he couldn't spot her anywhere. In that moment, he knew with gut-wrenching certainty how much he loved her— so much that he felt sick with fear.

Two of the over-the-wall crew lay on the ground. One, who'd been tripped up by the barricade, was slowly regaining his feet. Another, about three yards away from the first, was rubbing his knee. Because of their helmets—and his absolute terror that he'd soon see Stacy on the ground—Nathan couldn't tell who among the crew was hurt. Before he could even think clearly, a track medic was on the scene. Beside the medic was Stacy. She was unscathed.

"Thank you, God," he murmured.

Though his first impulse was to go to her, Nathan stayed back to let those trained to deal with the situation sort it out. The pit road was cleared of the wrecked cars and debris, and the medic conducted triage. The injured crew members had removed their helmets. Calvin Glass, the front tire carrier, still clutched his knee, and Stephens, the catch can man, was the one who'd been tripped.

After a quick word with Harley and Perry, Stacy stepped back by Nathan.

Without thought, Nathan tipped her face up to his. "Tell me you're fine."

"Not a scratch on me," she assured him.

Her face was pale and her blue eyes wider than ever, and he burned to pull her into his arms and keep her safe. Not that she'd allow that. He let his hand fall to his side and tried to keep the distance that she preferred between them.

"This is a mess," she said. "Calvin wasn't even touched, but thinks he messed up an old knee injury as he was moving away. He's not going to be back today, for sure."

"How about Stephens?"

She shook her head. "He didn't see it coming, but he says it probably looked worse than it felt. With all the safety equipment he was wearing, he's not badly hurt. The only problem is that he landed funny on his right hand. The medic says that his wrist isn't broken, but it sure as heck looks sprained."

"Not so great for a catch can man," Nathan said. Those gas cans were over eighty pounds apiece. One-handed, there was no way to help the gas man, keep the catch can to the overflow vent, plus make any required adjustments to the rear track bar. Stephens was out, too.

Harley and Perry joined them. Both men's faces were set in somber lines.

"How's Kent doing?" Nathan asked Perry. "Did he see any of this?"

"He's holding third right now. He knows what happened, that no one is seriously hurt, and that his job is to win this race," Perry replied. "Ours is to give him the chance to do that."

"Sid Cochran's going to get penalized beyond a one second stop 'n go for being too fast on pit road," Harley said. "Doesn't make a danged bit of difference to us, though. He wouldn't have caught Kent, anyway, and we're still banged up."

"What's the game plan?" Stacy asked him. "We have Merritt, the eighth man, but that still leaves another spot to fill."

Harley looked around. "Eldrige is out sick, which means that we don't have anyone here in support crew who's trained for over-the-wall. I did it, but that was ten years and ten pounds ago."

It was probably more like fifteen years and thirty pounds, but Nathan figured now wasn't the time to nitpick.

"We've got a minimum of two pits to go," Perry said. "You have about sixty laps before the next one to work this out and make it seamless. Think you can do it, Harley?"

"Yes," Stacy said, in the face of everyone else's silence.

Perry walked away, turning his full attention to the action on the track.

"So, other than me suiting up, what's your solution?" Harley asked Stacy.

"I don't have it yet, but I will," she replied. "I've got too much riding on this not to." After a moment's hesitation she asked Harley, "What about someone from Castillo's team?"

He shook his head. "They've already got their eighth man and another fill-in working in their over-the-wall pit crew. One of their regulars is out sick and another quit. They're stretched thinner than we are."

"Great," Stacy muttered.

An idea hit Nathan, one that was so horrible that it nearly circled back around to brilliant.

"I can do it," he said.

Stacy shot him an "are you *crazy?*" look. The answer to that was "probably certifiable."

"You can do this?" Harley asked.

"I'm sure I can. Put Merritt in for Calvin, and put me in as catch can man. I've done it with the crew, before."

"When?" Stacy asked.

"About a week after you tried Calvin's job," he replied. "I needed to know that you couldn't necessarily kick my butt at everything, and as it turned out, I was right. I tried each of the positions and beat you at front tire carrier, too."

She looked a little irked.

"Hey, I'm telling you to let you know I can pull it off, not to rub your nose in it."

"I know. It's not that. I just can't believe I'm in this position. Two more stops like the first two, and this job would have been mine."

"I can't promise you they'll go like the first two, but I can promise you that I'm the best choice we have."

She scanned the crew as if hoping that a fully trained over-the-wall man might materialize.

"I know you are," she said.

"And I'll do my best for the team." *And for you,* he wanted to add.

"Thank you," she said. "That's all I can ask."

"There's extra gear in the hauler," Harley said. "You'll have to get Stephens's gas apron from him, though."

"I'll take that as a yes," Nathan said.

"Once I clear it with Perry and the NASCAR official, it's a go. Just start getting ready."

Nathan took off at a sprint for the hauler. As he suited up, he concluded that he had two choices in front of him: hero or goat. Nathan chose hero. He just hoped like heck that fate wasn't choosing goat.

CHAPTER SIXTEEN

"GIFT WRAPPER," STACY muttered to herself. "Candy store clerk…"

She could think of countless stress-free jobs she could be doing, but instead, here she was…smack in the middle of Stress Central.

"I heard that you had a crew incident. Nothing ever happens the easy way for you, does it, kid?" she heard her brother ask from behind her.

Stacy turned and looked him up and down. "You're telling me that it does for you?"

A smile slowly worked its way across Kane's features. "You've got a point." He hitched his thumb toward the track. "My guy has taken first place, and his over-the-wall pit crew looks like it will be taking up a hospital wing."

"Not funny," she said to her brother.

"Hey, I'm just trying to learn from you and find a little humor…not to mention distract you."

"Thanks, but you're going to have to try harder. I don't think I'm distractible right now, anyway," she said, keeping half her attention on Perry. He'd be calling in Kent soon. Too soon, as far as she was concerned.

Over by the wall, the over-the-wall pit crew—including Calvin and Stephens, who'd already been released from the infield care center—had circled around Nathan. She didn't know if they were giving him advice or sending one last prayer up to heaven. Both would be good.

"It's pretty bold of Nathan to have stepped in, don't you think?" Kane said. "It shows you what he's made of."

"You don't need to sing his praises to me," Stacy replied. "I love him, but—"

"Stop there," Kane said. "I need a moment to gloat. I knew you loved him."

"Great. Gloat away, but you might want to do it after this pit stop."

Drivers had been coming in over the past few laps. She knew that Kent and the other leaders would roll in soon, too. As she expected, Perry gave the word. Stacy's heart began to pound. She knew odds weren't exactly favoring a fast stop, but for Kent's sake—and Nathan's, too—she wanted to see this go well.

Kent pulled into the stall, and Stacy hit her stopwatch's button. She quickly saw that Merritt was filling in for Calvin perfectly. If she could just stop herself from checking out Nathan, she might not expire of anxiety, after all. But she had to look. Just *had* to!

"Wow," she breathed.

If she hadn't known it was Nathan under all that gear, she would have thought that she was observing any other catch can man in any other pit stop. The guys cleared the car, and Kent was off again. Stacy checked her watch.

"How was it?" Kane asked.

"Decent," Stacy replied. Their work had been a far cry from the artistry of the first two stops, but it hadn't been a disaster for the team. So long as Kent continued to drive smart, he'd be able to protect his lead.

Nathan approached. After he'd taken off his helmet, he asked Stacy, "Do I want to know the time?"

"Thirteen-one," she replied.

"It felt like five seconds flat. Five really lost seconds on my part." He was winded, which concerned her a little, but she knew that could as easily be from the adrenaline pumping through him as from the exertion.

"You looked good," she said.

"Thanks," he replied, running a hand through his hair. "I'll try to keep it tighter on the next one." One of the crew called his name. "Time to go get critiqued," he said to Stacy, and then was off.

The following laps passed in a blur. Kane moved on to visit with his other clients' teams. Kent still held the lead, but Justin Murphy was gaining on him. Stacy tried not to get too anxious as Harley and Perry had some intense discussions about Kent's fuel burn rate. The over-the-wall pit crew just went about their business, acting as though today was nothing out of the ordinary. She even heard them joking with Nathan. Stacy wished she could find the wellspring of calm that the guys seemed to have tapped.

"Last pit, if we stay under green," Harley called over to Stacy.

She closed her eyes and for one brief second willed every good thought she had about success and safety toward her guys. She might well have lost her dream job on today's twist of fate, but right now, that didn't matter.

Kent pulled in, and the guys were all over the car in a heartbeat. She watched as the basics took place, plus a few adjustments to the rear track bar through the car's back window, that Drew, the rear tire changer, helped Nathan with. She knew it took more time than it should have, but it looked as well planned out as possible.

When it was over, she checked her stopwatch. Twelve-eight! Yes, she knew that it wasn't enough to win her the job, but it was far better than she had expected.

Back on Stacy's side of the wall, with their equipment squared away, Nathan and the guys took a moment for a round of high fives. Even Perry broke his concentration long enough to give an approving nod in the crew's direction.

Nathan joined Stacy.

"That was a bear to do. I don't think I'm going to quit my day job," he joked.

Her heart lurched as she recalled that he'd already done just that. She glanced over at him and was startled by his suddenly grim expression. Stacy looked away. His emotions were not her issue, whether she wanted it that way or not. She turned her attention back to the oval.

The race turned into a duel among the top six cars, especially as most of the other contenders pitted for one last time and fell behind. Stacy looked over at Perry. His jaw was set and his arms were crossed over his chest. He had made his plan and he was sticking with it.

By Lap 398, only Zack Matheson and Trey Sanford were sticking with Kent. All of them had to be driving on fumes by now.

"Kent knows how to get the best out of that car," Nathan said from beside her.

Stacy wished she could just close her eyes until the checkered flag dropped, but she couldn't. It was close, so close that she wasn't sure she'd seen what she thought she had until the Cargill-Grosso team erupted in cheers.

Kent had won!

Around her, people were high-fiving and backslapping. Without thought, Stacy wheeled around to face Nathan.

"Amazing!" she cried. She raised her hand in the air, half-expecting him to give her a high five.

"No way," he said, looking at her with such hungry intent that she felt a little edgy.

She brought her hand back down. "What?"

Without saying another word, Nathan swept her into his arms. Then, before she could draw a breath to protest, he leaned her back into the most absolutely perfect and astonishing Hollywood kiss she'd ever had. She clung to him and kissed him back with everything she felt but could never say. By the time he set her back on her feet, she could hear her guys cheering, and she knew that it wasn't for Kent's win.

"And *that*," Nathan said after a few ragged breaths, "is what we have to talk about."

Yes, there was *that*.

LATE THAT NIGHT, Stacy nervously paced the confines of her bedroom while Nathan waited in the living room. She couldn't believe that she'd worked up the nerve to ask him back here, but the flight home to Charlotte had been no place to talk. Though they'd sat next to each other in the small charter jet, they'd been surrounded by the team…a tired, happy, and talkative team. And now, when she most needed to be bold, her confidence had gone walking.

"Are you okay in there?" Nathan called.

Stacy winced. "I'll be out in a minute. Promise!"

She had asked him to give her a moment not so she could change into something pretty and spray on perfume like a diva, but so she could shake off her nerves. And shake she did. Since a yoga session was out of the question, she tried for a silent scream, which at least she found funny enough while doing that she began to calm.

No matter how tonight turned out, at least Stacy would know that she hadn't run from intimacy. She would tell him how she felt about him, even if this was all they would ever have. After taking one quick look around her bedroom to make sure it was neat—just in case, of course—she rejoined Nathan, who had made himself at home on the sofa.

"Can I get you something to drink?" she offered.

He inclined his head toward the soft drink she'd already gotten him before escaping to the bedroom. "You already have."

"Oh. Well, right."

"Do you think you might come sit down?"

It beat standing there trying not to wring her hands, so she did.

"It was one incredible night, wasn't it?" she asked tentatively.

"One I'll never forget," he agreed.

How could she do this? How could she start saying all the things that she'd kept to herself for so very long…especially when curiosity and passion simmered between them as it did right now?

"The heck with it," she exclaimed, then got herself just where she wanted to be…wrapped around Nathan, her lips against his. She kissed him until nerves became hunger, and then hunger became all-out need.

Finally, Nathan eased out of their embrace.

"I think we'd better talk before we forget how," he said.

He settled her head against his shoulder, one hand absently playing through the now tousled strands of her hair. She relaxed into his warmth and acceptance.

"I'm sorry for going off the deep end the night you saw me with Kane," she said.

"You had a right to be upset," he replied.

"Yes, but not to refuse to listen. That was wrong, and I want to tell you why I reacted that way…not as an excuse, but so that you'll understand."

He drew her in a little tighter to him, then said, "Kane already told me about Brenda and your childhood."

She lifted her head to meet his eyes. "He did? When?"

"That night. I badgered him into it."

"That's surprising."

"That I would badger your brother?"

"No, that he would let you."

Nathan's chuckle rumbled through her, and she snuggled back against him. She was touched that Kane had cared enough to involve himself.

"Would it help to talk about Brenda?" Nathan asked.

"Not tonight," she said. She wanted tonight to be about happiness. And if they had nights past this, then she'd talk about Brenda. "Tonight I just want to thank you."

"For what?"

"For giving me a chance at Cargill-Grosso, for starters. I know that you had to have had people better qualified than I was…college graduates, and—"

He gave her a little squeeze. "Hey, you were the very best person for the job. You had an enthusiasm that none of the rest of them showed."

Smiling, she lifted her head again. "Really?"

"Really," he affirmed.

She gave him a brief kiss. "Thank you. I just want you to know that you've changed my life," she added as she settled back against him. "I've decided that it's time to take my game up a notch. I'm applying to UNC Charlotte for their exercise physiology program. If all goes well, I'll be starting my basic courses in the winter semester."

"I know you can do it," he said.

She settled her hand against his heart, taking comfort from its strong beat. "And now I know I can, too. If I can walk in and face a crew of men who want nothing to do with me, and in less than two weeks, have them willingly practicing yoga and running until they drop, I can do pretty much anything."

"That, you can."

Because she was about to venture further into what was left of their employer/employee relationship, Stacy swung her feet to the floor, sat back up and scooted away from him just a little.

"I know I fell short on the ten percent time drop, but even with everything that happened, I came darned close. I also know that if Cargill-Grosso won't have me, another team will, and—"

"Cargill-Grosso will have you," Nathan cut in.

"But—"

He shook his head. "I boxed you into that time drop commitment. I was ticked off to be stuck in a job and a place that, at that moment, I didn't want to be. I took it out on you, and I shouldn't have. Time drops are crucial, but that measurement shouldn't have been a noose around your neck. I'm sorry.

"Besides, if I were crazy enough to insist that you pack your bags tomorrow, no one would let you, Stacy. They love having you work with them. Even Harley has gotten to like you…in his own way."

She had to laugh at that. "So the job is mine?"

"Yes."

Finally! Somewhere inside, Stacy was doing a little victory lap of her own. On the outside, she knew she was grinning like a fool, too.

"Thank you," she managed to say past her smile.

"You are the best thing I did for Cargill-Grosso…and for myself."

"Thank you," she murmured. She didn't dare read too much into the second part of what he'd said. And the best way she could do that was to remind herself that soon he'd be gone. "So, when are you heading back to Boston?"

"You mean permanently?"

"Well, yes. Of course."

"That was the other thing we needed to talk about. I'm not."

"Not what?"

"Heading back to Boston permanently. I've decided to stay."

"What?"

Maybe she was losing her ability to understand the spoken word. She scrambled from the sofa to look at Nathan, and see if he appeared as crazy as he was sounding to her.

He smiled. "I said I'm staying in Charlotte. Look at the bright side. At least this way we'll have some time to work on our communication issues."

"You're staying?"

"Should I try saying it in another language?"

"No," she replied, attempting to scrape her mind back together. "English is fine. Really. So, when?"

Now he looked confused. "When, what?"

"When did you decide to stay?"

"I think it was outside tonight when your neighbor waved at me. I've taken a liking to her."

"You can't mean this."

He smiled. "It's not so sudden. My affection for Mrs. Lorenzo…or at least Mrs. Lorenzo's beautiful and amazing neighbor…has grown every time I've seen her."

She knew that Nathan was joking, but this was still too good to be true. Nothing in life worked out this easily for her.

"You've been working toward getting back to Boston, and now you're just ditching the plan?" she asked.

He reached out to her. "Would you sit back down? I like life better when I can touch you."

Still rattled, she sat far enough away that she could face him.

"To seriously answer your question, it hit me at the track today that the only one making me leave was me. And I don't want to leave. Until this year, I used to be a mapper…a planner. But where has mapping gotten me, anyway? It seems that some of the better times I've had are when the map is yanked away from me."

"And here I've spent years looking for my bearings," she said.

He took one of her hands between his. As he examined it, tracing a line across her palm and to the tip of one finger, then the next, he spoke. "My dad's death taught me one thing that in a way I'm lucky to have learned at such a relatively early age. We're pretty fragile creatures, Stacy. We like to pretend we're tough and can conquer men and machines bigger than we are, but in the end, we're all very, very human, and with not a lot of time to spend on the planet."

He closed his hand around hers, and she held it tight.

"I could go back to Boston and pick up where I left off, but what I'd be leaving behind is too big a price to pay. I'd be leaving a sport that I love, one that reminds me of my father, whom I miss very much. I'm not the disaffected kid I once was, and I can see why racing was my dad's passion. I'll never have the bug that strongly, but I don't want to give it up, either. If, one day, I could get Dean and Patsy to let me buy back even ten percent of Cargill-Grosso, that would be enough. What I can't seem to get enough of, though, is you…."

He drew her closer and kissed her once, then twice, both filled with an emotion that Stacy didn't dare name.

"So here's the roadmap, whether or not it quite works out this way," he said. "I need to have a strong presence in Boston over the next six months while my partner and I get that office running at full potential, but I plan to be here…and I mean right here, next to you…every weekend that I'm welcome."

"That would be all of them," she said.

He smiled. "Good. Once I have that office under control, I plan to open a Charlotte branch. This is a growing area, one where I can see picking up a lot of clients…even some in racing. This city—and NASCAR—have proved to be good parts of my life, Stacy…but not the best. You are the very best part. I've fallen in love with you. I want to be here, with you…where you so clearly belong…to give that love a chance to grow."

She had so much that she wanted to say—that, yes, she loved him, too, and, yes, she wanted him in her life, night and day, forever—but she couldn't seem to get the words past the joy bubbling inside her. She held tighter to their linked hands.

"But nothing from you?" Nathan asked. "Maybe I've just been imagining what I've felt in our kisses?"

He'd spoken so tenderly that she knew he was certain of her love for him…as he should be.

She smiled. "You haven't imagined a thing. And I'm sure we'll talk about love until dawn. But first, there's more than one way to communicate, you know."

His returning smile was so sexy, so intimate, that she felt a little weak-kneed, which made her next move a challenge.

Stacy stood and drew him to his feet.

"Welcome home, my love," she said.

Her hand still clasped in his, Stacy led Nathan to her bedroom, where she planned to let him know in word and deed how thoroughly he was loved. After all, hard-won victories were all the sweeter to savor.

* * * * *

*For more thrill-a-minute romances
set against the exciting backdrop
of the NASCAR world, don't miss
NO HOLDS BARRED by Marisa Carroll
Available in June*

For a sneak peek, just turn the page!

"ETHAN? DO YOU HAVE a moment?" The voice of Maria Salinas, the Sanford Racing receptionist, sounded hesitant as it came through the intercom speaker on his desk.

"What is it?" Ethan winced at the impatience in his voice. It wasn't Maria's fault he was in a bad mood. Adam Sanford had just shot down his request for an extra weekend of testing at Kentucky. Too expensive. Nothing left in the budget this season for an unscheduled test session, he'd said.

Money. It always came down to money these days. Money—or the lack of it. Sure, his team owner had provided him with some of the best software available, but at the end of the day computer simulations, no matter how sophisticated, didn't take the place of a driver behind the wheel of his car. He needed Trey Sanford's input for the next phase of retooling his underperforming car—up close and personal—butt in the seat, hands on the wheel, not sitting in front of a big-screen TV playing high-tech video games.

"I said you have a visitor." There was an odd note in Maria's tone, as though she were torn between laughing and calling for help.

"I don't have any more appointments for today," he

said. "Get their name and tell them I'll call them later if it's important."

"I don't think this lady is going to take no for an answer." There was a short, charged moment of silence and then Maria's voice, from a distance, calling, "Wait. You can't go in there."

Ethan didn't even have time to hang up the phone before the door swung open unceremoniously and Mia Connors entered his office for the second time that day.

He blinked and took another look. No. It wasn't Mia Connors, but someone obviously closely related to his daughter's new nanny. This woman was slightly shorter, slightly heavier, with curves in all the right places. Her hair was darker than Mia's as well, a rich golden-brown that waved softly around her shoulders, held back from her face by a pair of tortoiseshell combs. And her eyes. They were different, too: hazel with flecks of gold and green and brown floating in their depths, just slightly elongated at the edges, giving her a faintly feline look, sleek, well fed, purring contentedly on your lap—until you crossed her.

He was looking at Mia's older sister, he guessed, the former marine.

"Ethan Hunt?" she said in a forceful tone banishing any further resemblance to a placid tabby cat. "I'm Cassandra Connors. Mia Connors's sister. I'd like to talk to you, if I may." She stood very straight, her shoulders back, her jaw thrust forward. She was wearing a calf-length cotton skirt and a short-sleeved V-neck sweater in a color he could best describe as kind of strawberry-red that just matched the angry flush on her cheeks.

"What can I do for you, Ms. Connors?" From the

look on her face she wasn't here to heap praise on his head for hiring her sister.

"I'm here to ask why you withdrew your offer to my sister of a job as a mechanic here at the race shop?"

He was right. She was here to do battle for her little sister. He couldn't fault her for that. He had done battle for both his sisters in the past.

"Won't you have a seat, Ms. Connors?" he asked.

"No, thank you. What I want is for you to reconsider your earlier decision."

"I'm afraid that's not possible, Ms. Connors."

"Why not? I'm not an expert on NASCAR, but it seems to me a certified NASCAR mechanic and a child's nanny are not interchangeable job descriptions. Am I correct, sir?"

"You are correct."

"My sister needs to be looking for a job in her chosen field, not helping you out of a jam by babysitting your daughter while you dangle the *possibility* of hiring her somewhere down the line." Her tone was perfectly even and devoid of heat, but the emphasis on the word was unmistakable.

"Mia's employment has been exemplary. We're happy with her work," he said. "Unfortunately, Sanford Racing is not hiring at this particular time."

She ignored his compliment on her sister's work ethic. "Where is your daughter?"

He was a little riled himself now. The Marine Corps mascot was a bulldog, he recalled suddenly. It was certainly an appropriate symbol for this particular marine. "She's in the break room having a snack. Not that it's any of your business."

"On the contrary," she said, not backing down an inch. "Since you coerced my sister into taking a job as her nanny, it is my business."

"I did not coerce your sister into anything," he responded, ignoring the tug of his conscience as he spoke. He hadn't coerced Mia, not exactly. She was an exemplary employee, and a damned good mechanic. He'd have hired her permanently in a heartbeat if he could. He wasn't proud of himself for manipulating the girl into becoming Sadie's nanny, but he was a desperate man. "The long and short of it is Sanford Racing doesn't have an opening for a mechanic at this time," he said bluntly.

"Then that makes what you did even worse. You have no intention of ever hiring my sister into this shop, correct?"

"I did not say that, Ms. Connors. I intend to keep my word. I want her on the team. I thought my suggestion would be a solution to both our problems—continued employment for Mia, a responsible nanny for my daughter. She agreed to the proposition." It was time to end this discussion before it escalated into an argument. He couldn't believe how this woman was pushing his buttons. He never let that happen. A gentleman didn't argue with women. He remembered his mother, his real mother, telling him that, in her soft, whispery voice. "Mia accepted my offer of her own free will. If she's changed her mind, then I need to hear that from her own mouth. Now, if you'll excuse me, Ms. Connors. I'll see you to the door. I have work to do."

Cassandra took a step closer to his big metal desk and leaned her hands on the scratched and dented surface.

He wasn't going to get rid of her that easily.

Copyright © 2009 by Harlequin S.A.

HARLEQUIN

//// NASCAR

Marisa Carroll
NO HOLDS BARRED

Sanford Racing crew chief Ethan Hunt needs a nanny, so he hires ex-marine Cassie Connors. Cassie knows how to take care of herself and her loved ones. She also knows how to go after what she wants—and she wants Ethan. Which means convincing the workaholic single father to gamble on a future where neither of them holds anything back.

*Available June 2009
wherever books are sold.*

www.GetYourHeartRacing.com

NASCAR18524R

HARLEQUIN®

//////// NASCAR

Bethany Campbell
ONE TRACK MIND

Longing to save her family's race track, Lori Garland is thrilled when a last-minute buyer makes an offer on the debt-ridden property—until she learns the mystery buyer is sports agent Kane Ledger, the bad-boy rebel she once loved and lost. Working together reopens old wounds… and rekindles undeniable desire. Can Kane and Lori become the winning team they were meant to be?

Available August 2009
wherever books are sold.

www.GetYourHeartRacing.com

NASCAR18525

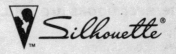

V *Silhouette*®

SPECIAL EDITION™

Emotional, compelling stories that capture the intensity of living, loving and creating a family in today's world.

Special Edition features bestselling authors such as Susan Mallery, Sherryl Woods, Christine Rimmer, Joan Elliott Pickart— and many more!

For a romantic, complex and emotional read, choose Silhouette Special Edition.

V *Silhouette*®

Visit Silhouette Books at www.eHarlequin.com   SSEGEN06

Whitney Maxwell is
about to get a lesson in
trust—and family—from
an unexpected source:
her student Jason. As
she and his single dad,
Dr. Shane McCoy, try to
help Jason deal with his
autism, she realizes her
dream of a forever family
is right in front of her.

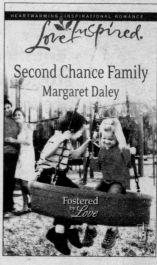

Look for

Second Chance Family

by

Margaret Daley

Available July
wherever books are sold.

www.SteepleHill.com

Steeple
Hill®

LI87535

Love Inspired HISTORICAL

INSPIRATIONAL HISTORICAL ROMANCE

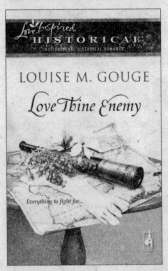

The tropics of colonial Florida are far from America's Revolution. Still, Rachel Folger is loyal to Boston's patriots, while handsome plantation owner Frederick Moberly is faithful to the crown. For the sake of harmony, he hides his sympathies until a betrayal divides the pair, leaving Frederick to harness his faith and courage to claim the woman he loves.

Look for

Love Thine Enemy

by

LOUISE M. GOUGE

Available July wherever books are sold.

Steeple
Hill®

www.SteepleHill.com

LIH82815

HARLEQUIN®

NASCAR

Ken Casper
RUNNING WIDE OPEN

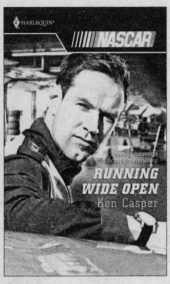

When an accident lands NASCAR driver Trey Sanford in the care of Dr. Nicole Foster, everything he's worked for is suddenly at risk. He will do whatever it takes to protect his family legacy…and his own carefully guarded secret. Nicole knows it would be tough for Trey to go public with his medical condition. He's already a hero to her kid brother. Maybe she can convince him that he is also a champion in her eyes.

Available October wherever books are sold.

www.GetYourHeartRacing.com

NASCAR18527

HARLEQUIN®

//////NASCAR®

Dorien Kelly
A TASTE FOR SPEED

Retired NASCAR champion Steve Clayton continues to take risks in everything—except love. Then he meets Sarah Stanton, a fiercely independent college professor who is totally different from any other woman he's met. Sarah has given up on love and knows the former NASCAR driver and paparazzi-loving playboy is completely wrong for her…so why is she so captivated when he continues to pursue her?

Available October wherever books are sold.

www.GetYourHeartRacing.com

NASCAR18528